For Jennings—mentor and friend
Thank you for laughing in all the right places.

THE Awesome, ALMOST 100% TRUE ADVENTURES OF Matt & Craz

WRITTEN AND ILLUSTRATED BY
ALAN SILBERBERG

Aladdin

NEW YORK LONDON TORONTO SYDNEY NEW DELHI

ALADDIN

An imprint of Simon & Schuster Children's Publishing Division
1230 Avenue of the Americas, New York, NY 10020
First Aladdin paperback edition April 2014
Text and illustrations copyright © 2013 by Alan Silberberg
All rights reserved, including the right of reproduction in whole or in part in any form.
ALADDIN is a trademark of Simon & Schuster, Inc.,
and related logo is a registered trademark of Simon & Schuster, Inc.
Also available in an Aladdin hardcover edition.
For information about special discounts for bulk purchases, please contact
Simon & Schuster Special Sales at 1-866-506-1949 or business@simonandschuster.com.
The Simon & Schuster Speakers Bureau can bring authors to your live event.
For more information or to book an event contact the Simon & Schuster
Speakers Bureau at 1-866-248-3049 or visit our website at www.simonspeakers.com.
Designed by Karin Paprocki
The text of this book was set in Archer Book.
Manufactured in the United States of America 0314 OFF
2 4 6 8 10 9 7 5 3 1
The Library of Congress has cataloged the hardcover edition as follows:
Silberberg, Alan
The awesome, almost 100% true adventures of Matt & Craz / written and illustrated
by Alan Silberberg. 1st Aladdin hardcover ed.
Summary: A weird web site provides Kilgore Junior High students and
best friends Matt and Craz the opportunity to make their cartoons become real,
which has some unexpected and dire consequences.
[1.Cartoons and comics—Fiction. 2. Magic—Fiction. 3.Junior high schools—Fiction.
4. Schools—Fiction. 5. Family life—Fiction. 6.Humorous stories—Fiction]. I. Title.
PZ7.S5798 Awe 2013   [Fic]   2012015554
ISBN 978-1-4169-9432-9 (hardcover)
ISBN 978-1-4169-9433-6 (pbk)
ISBN 978-1-4424-5183-4 (eBook)

UH-OH

IF MATT WAS A BETTER CARTOONIST AND CRAZ hadn't been dropped on his head as a baby, the gym wouldn't be a gigantic beehive. The student council would still be populated by humans. And a horde of pirates wouldn't be sword-fighting with Mrs. Bentz, a decent enough lady, but a terrible English teacher.

Unfortunately, Matt's no Picasso and Craz can't stop making stuff up, which is why they're both hiding inside a locker, desperately trying to come up with a plan to get Kilgore Junior High back to normal.

On the plus side—they don't have to hand in their English assignments.

2

LAST TUESDAY

"COME ON, TURKLE," CRAZ SAID, WAVING THE
rectangular sheet of paper like a flag he wanted to
plant in the newspaper editor's skull. "Don't be such a
jerk. It's funny."

Skip Turkle didn't have a funny bone in his body. He
was 150 pounds of super-suck-up and made decisions

based on what would look good on his college transcripts, something he'd been doing since second grade. "Funny is three panels with a punch line." Turkle reached for the single-panel cartoon in Craz's hand, which he crushed into a tight ball. "This . . . is a waste of paper."

"And ink!" sprang the whiny voice of Diesel McKenzie, star cartoonist of the Kilgore Junior High *Lantern*, who just happened to be Skip Turkle's best friend.

"Yes," replied Turkle, never one to miss the chance to make Craz feel even worse. "And ink. High-five!"

Craz watched Turkle slap the mole-size palm that Diesel held up. At four-foot-eight, McKenzie was the shortest kid in the grade, which in a normal universe would've made him an easy target for every taller kid in the school. But Diesel Mckenzie was actually a pretty decent cartoonist, which gave him a boost where the lifts in his sneakers didn't.

"Better luck next time," Diesel spat out at Craz. "And tell Matt his lines are droopy."

"Yeah, droopy," added Turkle, trying unsuccessfully to hold in his snort of a laugh that made him look like a pig with indigestion.

"How can a line be droopy?" Matt was halfway through the peanut butter and potato chip sandwich that was his Tuesday staple. Five days, five sandwiches. That was his lunchtime motto.

MONDAY—tuna fish and pickles.

TUESDAY—the already mentioned (and chewed) peanut butter and chips.

WEDNESDAY—roast beef on a naked bun.

THURSDAY—bacon and mayo with extra bacon.

FRIDAY—sandwich surprise.

Matt Worfle liked order. Socks had to match. Schedules needed to be made and met. Lunch had to be eaten in sequence. Predictable. Edible. It worked for his life and his stomach.

Craz, on the other hand, took pride in being all over the place. He could eat an entire box of Froot Loops for lunch one day and then snarf down a whole barbecue chicken the next. Out-of-order was his order, and it was something that he was actually really good at.

"I know Turkle is *Lantern* editor, but since when is it his job to judge our stuff?" Craz had rescued the balled-up cartoon he and Matt had made, and he now smoothed it out onto the cafeteria table, carefully avoiding the bomb of peanut butter that fell from Matt's mouth.

"Sorry to break it to you, Craz, but that's what an editor does—hands out assignments and holds the hatchet for what lives and dies inside the paper."

"But 'Kitty Litter' is funny." Craz loved the cartoons he and Matt came up with. Sure, they were gross and stupid. That was the whole point. "Who wouldn't laugh at a lazy, poop-eating cat?"

Matt took another bite of his sandwich. "You got me, bro," he said. "Cat eating poop. Nothing funnier than that."

"Kitty Litter" was just one of the dozens of doomed comic strip ideas that sprang from Matt's and Craz's bizarro minds. "Melvin Gherkin—Pickle Boy," "Seasick and Slaphappy," "Butt-Ugly Bob," and "The Adventures of Mary the Meatball Sub" were some of the other twisted ideas the two friends had tried unsuccessfully to get printed in the school paper.

"We're ahead of our time," Craz kept saying every time another cartoon was handed back with a bright red REJECTED stamped on the envelope.

Matt was much more of a realist. "We're not ahead of our time," he told his friend. "We're just weird."

"Weird is good."

"Not if we want to get printed in the *Lantern*. This is junior high, Craz. And weird . . . is just *weird*."

Matt drained his chocolate milk container, purposely leaving a milk mustache that he then licked off. "Oh, well," he said as he smoothed the crinkled edges of the "Kitty Litter" cartoon before sliding it carefully into the growing "reject" folder inside his backpack. "Back to the drawing table."

"You don't have a drawing table," Craz said, wolfing down Matt's last bite of sandwich.

"Maybe that's the problem." Matt laughed. "I just don't have the right supplies."

"If only!" Craz said, his crooked smile showing off the gob of peanut butter stuck to his gums. "That would make life *way* easier!"

The school bell rang, putting an end to lunch but not their hope. Craz and Matt weren't giving up. They'd find a way to get their cartoons printed with or without Skip and Diesel's help.

3

TOO MUCH NOISE

THE MUSIC WAS SO LOUD THAT MATT HEARD IT before stepping off the bus. He hesitated on the bottom stair, instantly wanting to run back to his seat and ride the number 23 all the way to the end of the line and just stay there. Forever. Unfortunately, the last time he tried hiding out on the bus, he got caught by the driver, who ended up making an angry phone call to his mother. And she was not happy that she had to drive all the way to the Rutland bus yard to pick him up.

Matt had no choice but to let the reverberating bass line and screeching lyrics reel him in toward his house.

Judging by the decibel level of the music, his mother was still at work, which meant his older brother, Ricky, was home alone with five or twenty of his high school friends, eating whatever food was in the fridge and making a mess that no one would ever clean. In Matt's house, chaos teetered between dirty laundry baskets, and the growing piles were glaciers that swallowed furniture and surfaces whole.

It used to be that he'd come home from school to the smell of fresh-baked cookies and a hug from his mother, who'd only worked part-time at her banking job. Of course, now Matt was too big for hugs, but that didn't stop him from wishing things hadn't changed so much at home. Standing on the front steps, he could picture the scene inside, and he wished he could just use a big fat eraser to make it all go away.

"Look who's home," yelled Foomer, Ricky's best friend, who Matt thought looked like a color-blind baboon that'd been let loose in a Gap store.

A couch pillow smacked Matt in the chest, knocking his sketchbook to the floor. As usual, Foomer was in perfect form. "Look alive. You dropped the pass, doofus!"

Matt pushed through the tangle of kids scattered throughout his living room, carefully avoiding the sneakers that tried to trip him, and doing his best not to choke on the body-odor stink.

"Where's Ricky?" he asked Foomer, whose freakish shrug enforced the baboon image already in Matt's brain. Matt made a mental note to draw Foomer as soon as he got to the safe haven of his room.

Wading his way through the jungle of Ricky's obnoxious friends, Matt worried that he had no way of escaping the curse that seemed to turn normal junior high kids into nasty high school jerks. Ricky used to be the best older brother in the world. Matt could always count on the fact that if he needed help in any way, his older bro would have his back. But as soon as Ricky hit ninth grade, everything changed. No more all-night slasher movie fests or bike rides to Dairy Queen for Oreo Blizzards. Ricky had torn off his Superman costume and tossed it and his younger brother under a bus.

Sure, Ricky's ninth grade was also the year their parents split up, and maybe that had something to do with the change. But if Mrs. Petrone, Matt's health teacher, was right, "growing up is a work in progress," which meant the possibility still existed that Ricky could grow back into the brother that Matt missed.

Being surrounded by Ricky's gang of guys always made Matt even more aware that he didn't have a "gang." All he had was Craz. And even though Craz had the personality of ten kids, Matt sometimes wished his social circle wasn't just a line.

"Incoming!" Foomer's voice preceded the splat of cold spaghetti that landed on Matt's head. Foomer's ape paw came next, and he rubbed the tomato sauce wig into Matt's scalp. "Nice fro, bro!"

Matt fumed, wishing his brother would step in and stand up for him. But as usual Ricky just laughed at Foomer's idiotic antics. "Foomer, you should go to art school. You sure can make a mess look good."

Matt wanted to say something but knew any attempt at retaliation would be a waste of time. And so he headed down the hallway, leaving strings of spaghetti in his wake until he got to the one place where no one could bother him: his desk.

NEW IDEA

WUZZUP?

Zip. U?

Ditto.

Craz was at his computer, typing with one hand while the other clutched a frozen burrito, which he ate like a Popsicle. He loved how the cold layers melted slowly, creating a fiesta of flavors in his mouth.

K where were we? Craz typed with his index finger. *O yeah. Nano-Second Newton...*

He was just about to share his latest cartoon idea about a kid who could freeze time, when a tundra-size chunk of cheese fell out of the burrito and onto his keyboard.

Ooops. brb...

Unlike Matt, who didn't dare allow food or drink within a five-foot radius of his computer, Craz's desktop policy was more like an all-you-can-eat buffet. Cans of soda, hot soups, icy frozen entrees, were all fine by him. The worst that could happen had already happened too many times to count. Keyboard or motherboard, Craz was a technical whiz who could fix any of the food-related error messages he caused.

And so a blob of burrito on his keyboard was nothing more than a slight detour in the conversation. With surgeonlike precision Craz rescued the melting jalapeño-cheddar cube from between the delete and + keys, then tossed it into his mouth.

"Tasty," he said as he wiped his fingers on his pants, adding a new stain to compete with the others already there.

U still on? Craz typed out, his fingers just slightly goopy.

Here, Matt answered. *Whatcha got?*

Excited, Craz shoved the whole burrito between his teeth, freeing up both hands to better type out the idea

that had come to him while showering before school earlier that day.

Craz's best ideas always came to him in the shower.
In a perfect world he would give up school and spend
every day just dreaming up cartoons underneath a
steady stream of hot, pulsating water.

Unfortunately, bathroom time in the Crazinski home
was a commodity not to be wasted, especially in the
morning, when five kids competed for the attention of
one groaning bathroom. Becca, his oldest sister, always
got the first shower. Then came Hank, Craz's sixteen-
year-old brother. Pete and Meagan, his little brother and
sister, fought to go next, which left Craz to take the last
shower. Always last.

It was such a logistical nightmare that Craz's dad
had to create an elaborate schedule that gave each kid a
total of 3.5 showering minutes before the hot water tank
quickly ran from hot to warm to freezing cold. This was
why a white kitchen timer shared space with wedges of
soap and bottles of shampoo. One sibling hogging even
twenty extra seconds caused a domino effect, which
made the last kid's shower a frozen nightmare.

It was in such a moment, when the shower had suddenly spat out an ice-cold spray, that Craz had instantly come up with the idea of Nano-Second Newton, a character who could freeze time and do anything he ever wanted. Like take a really, really long hot shower.

Try this—Newton is just a regular kid who has too many things to do, Craz typed out. *Then one day he gets this power...*

How? Something he eats? Matt typed back.

No no no... It's got to connect better. Like Peter Parker. He gets the spider bite and then—ZAP—dude is Spider-Man!

Ok ... So Newton gets time-stopping power from, I dunno... a cursed alarm clock? A bite from a radioactive stopwatch?

ROFL! I like the stopwatch. ... Maybe he finds an antique stopwatch...

Could it belong to his father? wrote Matt.

Sounds good 2me. Maybe his dad hid it because he was about to be captured... By time gypsies!

I like it! And it has powers... because it was built by...

Chronos!! Greek god of time!

Yes!!!!!!!!!!!!

If they could've high-fived over the Internet, they would have. Instead Matt celebrated by grabbing a blank piece of paper and his favorite ballpoint pen, while Craz just popped the rest of the melting burrito into his smiling mouth. Sure, there was a better chance of them actually being able to freeze time than getting "Nano-Second Newton" printed in the school paper. But they didn't care. They just loved making up new cartoons together.

We rock!

Totally!!!!

Sheltered in his room, Matt was already doodling the character of Newton, a dorky kid with an overbite

and a mysterious stopwatch, while halfway across town Craz paced the cramped room he shared with his two brothers, busy writing the story that would bring the new character to life.

It was the hardest part, the most exciting part, and for the two best friends who pushed aside their homework to do the work they loved, it was going to be a late night.

5

SCHOOL STINKS

KILGORE JUNIOR HIGH HAD DEFINITELY SEEN
better days. Bricks routinely fell from the facade, and
windows that swelled in the heat remained stuck in
whatever position they'd last been. The classrooms
hadn't seen a fresh coat of paint in decades and were
cursed with the smell of ancient BO, while the auditorium had more broken chairs than working ones. Even
the football field, home of the Kilgore Killer Bees, was
a mess, dotted with ruts that seemed to swallow frail
students whole.

It was the oldest school in town, which was a source
of pride for anyone who didn't have to go there. Unfortunately, Matt and Craz did have to go there. And neither

was doing particularly well. They were both C-average kinds of guys. Matt's mom was always on him to bring his grades up, something he knew he could do if he only tried. But classroom time was doodling time, and Matt's notebooks were more full of cartoons than actual notes. He couldn't help himself. When he saw blank space on a sheet of paper, he had to fill it with whatever images floated into his brain. It was almost as if his pen had a mind of its own that made the squiggles and dots turn into his funny little doodles.

Craz, on the other hand, tried as hard as he could and still wound up with so-so grades. Luckily, being the middle kid in a large family meant his report cards slipped through the cracks unnoticed, and aside from the occasional "Oh, Larry, C minus again?" there were never any real consequences to suffer back at home.

For Craz, math was a disaster. Science—a black hole of learning. And Craz was doing so poorly in French that his teacher had given up and just made him read Dr. Seuss's *Le Chat au Chapeau* every day. But if Matt was wild about cartooning, Craz loved writing stories. Making stuff up was something he was good at, so English class should've been a no-brainer.

Sadly, when you have an English teacher as dull and mean as Mrs. Bentz, even your favorite subject can turn into prison time. Edna Bentz was shaped like an ostrich egg (something Matt had captured perfectly). Her wide eyes seemed to look in separate directions, and she had a voice that could grate potatoes.

MRS. BENTZ

"All the way in, Long John stood by the steersman and conned the ship. He knew the passage like the palm of his hand," Mrs. Bentz recited flatly. As usual she was reading from her favorite book, *Treasure Island*, by Robert Louis Stevenson. They'd been studying that book all year with painful page-by-page scrutiny, and to be honest the whole class was sea-sick of it. It didn't help that Mrs. Bentz's nasal, monotone voice made each word a painful experience, and since she insisted on being the only one to read aloud, it was all any of the kids could do to actually listen.

"And what was Mr. Stevenson implying with his imagery of the wide-open seas? Anyone? Someone?"

But no one bothered to raise a hand. The kids all knew there was no point in trying to make a point. Mrs. Bentz would shoot down any thoughtful or creative idea, making sure her students learned that learning, in her class, meant listening—not thinking. And so while each student did their best to avoid eye contact, Mrs. Bentz waited in silence, took a deep breath and finally continued.

"It's not like I enjoy reading this," she lied. And then, licking her plump finger to turn a page in the well-worn book, she said, "Well, I suppose if no one wants to join the discussion, I might as well continue." The whole class groaned in response and did their best to block out her voice until the bell rang.

Escape from Treasure Island

6

THE *LANTERN*

"AWESOME JOB, MATT," CRAZ SAID AS HE LOOKED
over the finished cartoon. "You did it again, my friend."

Matt stood by his locker, beaming. He'd been up
until four in the morning creating the finished comic
based on the idea that he and Craz had come up with.
"I gotta admit I wasn't sold at first. But I think this is the
one, Craz. 'Nano-Second Newton' is going to blow Turkle
away. He'll have to print it, right?"

"Yup," Craz replied as he slid the comic strip back
into the manila envelope that they would take down to
the *Lantern* office. "This time we're golden."

The school newspaper office was located in the

basement, sandwiched between the janitor's supply closet and the dark and stinky boys' bathroom that only the desperate kids used. The *Lantern* logo was stenciled on the opaque glass door, an image of an old-time lantern with a beam of light shining out. Also stenciled in bold black letters was the editor's name: Skip P. Turkle.

IT WAS WEDNESDAY LUNCHTIME, SO SKIP TURKLE was having his editorial meeting for Thursday's *Lantern* edition. Since becoming editor at the beginning of the year, Turkle had actually done a great job. The school paper used to only come out once a month. It had been a two-page snore fest that pretty much listed whatever Principal Droon wanted the students to know—who made honor roll, what was for lunch, the lamest jokes ever. But thanks to Turkle, the *Lantern* now had actual sections like sports, entertainment, news, and of course comics. And it wasn't just one issue a month. The *Lantern* now came out every Tuesday and Thursday and was staffed by a dozen kids who loved writing and reporting as much as they hated Skip Turkle. The truth was, Turkle was good with the paper—and bad with people. Really bad.

"Come on, Skip. It's a good story." Debbie Dewey stood by the editor's wide desk, waving a sheet of paper. Debbie was a nice enough eighth grader who liked writing human-interest stories. "Mrs. Millman was voted Teacher of the Year."

"Get real, Dewey," Skip said dismissively. "So she's a good teacher. Bore me now. N.N."

Debbie sat back down in defeat. She knew that once Skip gave you the dreaded "double N," you had zero chance of convincing him to run your story. "N.N." stood for "not news," and Skip handed it out like breath mints, which was something he could sure make good use of.

Leaning back in his chair, Skip draped his feet on his desk and cracked his knuckles, knowing that at least half of his staff had repeatedly begged him not to. "Diesel, what do you have for tomorrow?"

Staff cartoonist Diesel McKenzie rose from his seat and walked up to the editorial desk. Short and lean, McKenzie was a miniature version of a good-looking kid. With dark brown eyes and hair that knew exactly where to go, he had a killer smile and teeth worth every cent his orthodontist was paid. His physical shortage was helped by his confidence, which seemed to add at least two inches to his challenged height.

"Here you go, boss," McKenzie said as he tossed a horizontal sheet of paper across the desk. "How do you like my latest *Little Big Shots*?"

Diesel did occasional editorial cartoons, but *Little Big Shots* was the comic strip that he'd been drawing for the *Lantern* since Skip Turkle had taken over as editor.

It was a well-drawn three-panel comic featuring an odd-ball assortment of little kids who acted much older than they really were. It wasn't particularly funny, and it was never shocking or mean. No one complained about it. No one raved about it. It was the kind of cartoon someone's parents would clip out and put on the refrigerator, which made a kid like Diesel grin with the satisfaction of a job well done.

LITTLE BIG SHOTS by Diesel McKenzie

Turkle looked over the pen-and-ink comic and started nodding excitedly. "Good stuff, Diesel. Real good."

MATT AND CRAZ STOOD OUTSIDE THE *LANTERN* office door rehearsing what they wanted to say. Well, not exactly what they *wanted* to say, but what they *thought* they should say. What they *wanted* to say was, "Listen up, Turkle. Your gigantic ego is out of control, and it's time you stopped keeping our funny cartoons out of your brain-dead rag of a paper."

Craz knew they couldn't really say anything like that. What they should say would have to be much less—what was the word?—truthful!

"Ready?" asked Craz.

"Does it matter? Let's just do this." Matt gave his friend a thumbs-up.

Craz nodded and then gripped the doorknob, took a deep breath, and plastered a big smile onto his face as he pushed the door open.

"Look what seeped out of the janitor's closet," Turkle said before they could even step inside.

The boys stood in the cramped newspaper office, uncomfortable and already on the spot.

Diesel piped up like a tiny squirrel. "You two really are gluttons for punishment, aren't you?" And then, seeing the manila envelope in Matt's hand, he said "Look, Skip. He's got another lame cartoon with him."

The envelope Matt was holding felt like it was starting to glow red-hot. Matt was seething on the inside, but he slid the envelope onto Skip Turkle's desk. "Just a new idea we came up with. Hope you like it." Matt smiled nervously and even laughed a little to make up for how uncomfortable he felt.

Diesel bounced up and down on his tiptoes, watching Skip's face to see what he would do. There's only room for one cartoonist on the *Lantern*, he thought. And that cartoonist is me!

Craz hummed a silent tune and Matt chewed a hang-nail off his thumb while they waited for Skip Turkle to react.

Turkle cracked his knuckles (again) and reached for the envelope. "New idea, huh?" He held the envelope in his open palm as if trying to guess what was inside. "We could always use some new ideas around here. Isn't that right, guys?"

The rest of the *Lantern* staff didn't know what to say. They were used to just going along with Turkle, but they also knew Turkle hated anything that Matt and Craz came up with.

Craz fidgeted some more. "Anyway, just wanted to see what you thought," he said. "Take your time."

Turkle slid his nail under the envelope clasp. "Why take my time when we can all use a good laugh now?"

Caught off guard, Matt said, "Now? Sure, now's good. And this cartoon is funny. Really funny!"

Diesel McKenzie's eyes began to water, which only happened when he was nervous. The rest of the staff sat quietly watching, wondering what their boss was going to do.

Skip Turkle reached into the envelope and slowly pulled out the crisp new drawing. Several writers leaned forward to try to get a peek but were stopped by Turkle's mean glare.

Turkle held the comic in front of him and looked down at it. A slow grin spread across his fat cheeks. It looked like he was enjoying the cartoon, thought Craz.

But that thought was short-lived. Skip Turkle spun around in his swivel chair, flicked on the paper shredder, and chuckled loudly as the cartoon was turned to confetti.

"Like I said, we could all use a good laugh. Pretty funny, huh?"

7

DRAW BETTER NOW

THE MICROWAVE HUM MEANT THE PIZZA POCKETS were almost ready. It had been a long day, and Matt and Craz were both ready to drown their sorrows in hot snack food, and lots of it.

"Why don't they make these babies stuffed with chocolate?" Craz asked while he stared at the plate going round and round inside the microwave.

"Beats me," said Matt from his seat at the kitchen table. "Maybe that's what we should do. Come up with new junk food ideas instead of wasting our time making stupid comics."

Craz looked over at his friend. Matt sat slumped in his chair, absently doodling on a napkin. He'd been sulking all day since Turkle had paper-shredded their new comic.

"Diesel and Skip are both total jerks. Like they share the same brain," Matt said, and then held up the napkin sketch of Diesel and Skip. "What do you think?"

Craz smiled. "Not bad. But I think you made their brain too big."

Matt nodded and then flipped the napkin over and instantly started redoing the cartoon.

DING! The pizza pockets were done. The timer bell brought Ricky and Foomer into the kitchen, their mouths open and drooling like rabid dogs.

"Food!" Foomer bellowed as he reached for the plate in Craz's hands.

"Nuke your own, Foomer," said Craz. "Even you could figure out how to do that."

Ricky laughed. "Good one, spaz. But I think you give Foomer too much credit."

"Yeah," said Foomer, who swatted dumbly at the plate again, trying in vain to grab one of the piping-hot pizza snacks. "Gimme."

Protecting his own plate from his older brother, Matt got up from the table and pulled on Craz's arm. "Come on, Craz," Matt said as Ricky tried to block him. "Let's hit my room."

Craz's face lit up. "*Food* in your room? Really? This is a special day."

MATT'S BEDROOM WAS LIKE ANOTHER PLANET compared to the rest of the Worfle house. It was almost as if his perfectly tidy room had been plucked from a sanitized parallel universe and then dropped into the chaos. His bed wasn't just made; the bedspread was smooth and tight like it had just had a face-lift. All of Matt's books were neatly lined up in his bookcases, and there wasn't one piece of clothing on the floor or dirty dish hidden behind the bureau.

Craz was always in awe of Matt's need to keep his stuff organized. Craz knew that in his room it was just a waste of time to put things where they belonged, not that he knew where anything was supposed to go. That's the upside of sharing a room with two brothers. The downside? Two brothers.

They sat at the computer watching stupid videos on YouTube. Though Matt had okayed bringing food into his room, he insisted that they obey the No Eating Zone around his computer, which meant Craz had to keep leaping up to grab a bite from his pizza pocket, which sat on the bookcase shelf.

"Why would anyone record their dog in a tutu?" Craz asked, slurping down a sloppy bite.

"Better question," replied Matt, his own plate out of reach. "Why would the dog agree to it?"

The clip of a Chihuahua dressed in a pink tutu chasing its own tail set to the theme from *Star Wars* was playing for the third time.

"Animals are strange."

"People are stranger," said Matt, clicking to another video. This one featured two babies seemingly having a discussion about hot girls. It was pretty ridiculous, which is why it had more than two hundred thousand hits.

Craz watched the clip for a second time, and his eyes lit up. "This gives me an idea for a new cartoon. 'Little Baby Big Butt'! What do you think? Talking babies with high IQs who burp and spit up while doing movie reviews and stuff!"

Matt was hardly excited. "I dunno, man. To be honest, I'm not sure I want to even try again."

"Come on, Matt," Craz said, trying to sound upbeat. "You wouldn't want things to be easy, would you?"

Matt sighed. "I could get used to easy."

This wasn't the first time Matt had felt like giving up after a cartoon had gotten rejected, and so Craz launched into one of his pep talks. "Don't forget, all great artists had to suffer a little. Look at that van Gogh dude."

Matt turned around to stare at his friend. "I like *both* my ears, thank you very much."

"Okay. Bad example, but you know what I mean. We can't give up now. We're so close."

"Close to what? I don't care about getting printed in the *Lantern* anymore." Matt rolled his chair over to the bookcase so that he could grab his pizza pocket. He took a bite and then rolled back to his desk.

A smile spread on Craz's lips. He had an idea. "You know what you need, Matt? Something to give you a creative kick in the pants. You always wished you had real cartooning supplies, right?"

Matt looked at his small desk, which had to double as a drawing table. Sure the surface was neat, but it wasn't the work space of a cartoonist. And his "supplies" amounted to a stack of cheap white paper and a clear drinking glass that held an assortment of chewed-on plastic pens. It was hardly a professional setup.

"Yeah, someday, maybe."

Craz pushed Matt away from the keyboard. "Not *some-day*, my friend. Today!" He cleared the YouTube page and opened up Google. *Cartoonist supplies*, he typed out with greasy fingers. "We're gonna hook you up, bro!"

"What are you doing?" asked Matt. "We can't afford stuff."

"No harm in looking," said Craz, while the list of search results popped onto the screen. "Besides, my grandmother just sent me some birthday cash. Maybe it's time to invest in our future."

The search page showed a long list of entries that linked to various art stores and online sites specifically devoted to cartooning. The screen was full of images of india inks that promised the blackest lines, fancy pen nibs that fit into sleek handcrafted pen shafts, smooth sheets of pearl-white bristol board used by the pros. Clicking through the links was like a fantasy window-shopping trip for Matt, who was used to drawing on scraps of paper meant for the trash, and whose most expensive pen cost two dollars, and that was because it came in a pack of two.

"I've got to admit it would be pretty cool to have some real supplies," said Matt. "I mean, my cartoons are okay the way they are, but with a real pen like that . . ." He was staring at the Bull's-eye Elite, a top-rated refillable fountain pen that came with an assortment of different-size drawing nibs. "Who knows what great stuff I could draw?"

Craz could tell he had gotten his friend excited again. "I think a new pen is exactly what you need. How much is that bad boy?"

Matt clicked on the price link. He gasped. "One hundred and fifty bucks? For a pen?"

Craz sank, deflated, onto Matt's neat bed. "That must be some pen," he said, knowing that all he had was twenty dollars. He'd figured on spending maybe half of it. But more than a hundred dollars? "That's out of my league, Matt."

"Yeah, that's just crazy." Matt exhaled loudly, letting the fantasy go. "It was a nice idea, though."

"Hold on," said Craz. He wasn't ready to admit defeat. "Maybe we can find something a little less . . . flashy." He took a bite from his pizza pocket while looking over

Matt's shoulder at a dozen different pens. They couldn't all cost so much. "Hey, how about that one?"

Craz pointed at a simple-looking pen that came with one nib point.

"You mean the purple one, right?" asked Matt, pointing to a pen near the top of the page.

"No, man. The black one," said Craz, now leaning over Matt and pointing out the pen he thought would be cheapest. Unfortunately, Craz had totally forgotten about the No Eating Zone, and his pizza pocket was now precariously suspended over Matt's keyboard.

Matt smelled it before seeing it happen. While Craz pointed at the computer screen, his pizza pocket gave birth to a chunk of cheesy pineapple, which hung for a second before falling directly onto the space bar. Sauce and pizza goop were everywhere.

"Craz!" Matt freaked out and reached for some tissues. "That's what I get for breaking my own rules." Frantic, he scrubbed the space bar and tried soaking up the wet sauce by jamming the tissue in between the surrounding keys.

While Craz stood helplessly in the background, Matt

cleaned the mess and then dropped the wet tissue into the trash. "You know what?" he said, and sighed. "This is all stupid. And I still think Skip Turkle is a pig!"

He grabbed the mouse and moved the cursor to shut down his computer. But instead of turning off, the screen lit up with a pop-up ad.

DRAW BETTER NOW! the rectangular ad read.

"Give me a break. Now what?"

"Must be an ad from one of the sites we visited," said Craz. "Just click off it."

Matt clicked on the *X* in the corner to close the annoying pop-up, but then three more identical windows opened up, each one shouting in bold caps, *DRAW BETTER NOW!*

"Stupid spambots," Matt said as he tried to navigate away from the evil ads, which now just kept multiplying on his screen. "I hate these things."

Craz tossed the last bite of his pizza pocket into his mouth, wiped his hands on his pants, and stepped next to Matt. "Okay, force quit. Try control-alt-delete."

"What do you think I'm doing?" Matt said, his fingers already spread across the keyboard in an effort to execute the kill command. The pop-up ads kept taking over the computer until Matt tried to force quit a second time. He smiled when there was a momentary hiccup on-screen that made all of the ad windows disappear. "Yes. It's working."

But instead of fixing things, the forced quit triggered something even worse. The screen went to black, leaving just the cursor blinking in the empty void.

"Dude, what did you do?" Craz said, leaning over Matt's shoulder. He grabbed the keyboard and repeatedly pressed the escape key. At first nothing happened, but a few seconds later the computer hummed and the empty screen gave way to a bright new web page. The page had a simple design and read, *Boyd T. Boone invites YOU to be the best cartoonist ever!* Beneath the words was a cheesy cartoon drawing of an artist in a smock and a beret, and a large blinking icon that read, *ENTER.*

"Enter?" asked Matt as he stared at the curious invitation. "Enter what?"

"Dunno," Craz said. He put his hand on his friend's shoulder. "But I'm ready to find out if you are."

8

THE WEBSITE

THE *ENTER* ICON BLINKED INVITINGLY.

"Here goes nothing," Matt said.

With a simple click of the mouse, a new web page loaded and the computer screen erupted into a spinning spiral of colors, while the tiny speakers on Matt's desk blared a music loop that sounded like it came straight from a circus sideshow.

Craz looked at the URL of the website. "www.draw-betternow.com?" Craz said. "What kind of a name is that?"

"Weird," Matt said as the colorful vortex drew him in. He tried to turn off the music, but no matter what he did, the annoying jingle just repeated over and over. "Ach! This music is terrible."

"Actually, I kind of like it," Craz said as he bounced along to the oompah blasts of the tuba. "Makes me want to smother my face in cotton candy."

The music suddenly stopped and the intro screen of twirling colors was replaced by a big, bold question set against a white background.

TIRED OF NO ONE SEEING YOUR CARTOONS? the question asked.

"Well, duh," said Craz. "Click the yes button."

Matt clicked yes, and the first question was replaced by a second one.

WISH YOU COULD BE A SUCCESSFUL CARTOONIST?

"Ditto on that one," Craz said. "Hey, I like these questions. They're easy."

Again Matt clicked yes, making a third question appear on the screen.

WANT TO BRING YOUR CARTOONS TO LIFE?

"*Bring my cartoons to life?* What's that mean?" asked Matt.

"Simple. It means make cartoons that are so awesome,

they jump off the page. The kind everyone likes. Even Turkle."

"Even Turkle," repeated Matt. "I like the sound of that."

Matt moved the cursor so that the word "yes" was highlighted. As soon as he clicked the mouse, the question disappeared, leaving just empty white space on the screen. The computer then hummed and whirred, and the boys could hear the CPU working overtime as the hard drive spun loudly inside the computer case.

"Now what?" asked Craz as a small video window popped open and started playing automatically.

In the video a wide man sat hunched over a drawing table. The bulky figure had his back to the camera while he worked wildly at some unseen drawing. His right hand clutched a pen that speedily drew across the sheet of paper in front of him, and his shiny bald head bounced along as his whole body became part of the motion of his drawing hand.

Suddenly the man just stopped, as if his batteries had run out. "Another masterpiece!" he declared, and then

spun around in his chair, clutching the finished drawing in his hands.

Matt and Craz stared at this bearlike figure, shoulders
slightly curved from too many hours at a drawing board.
His bare scalp and round face were accented by a big
bushy mustache, and two furry caterpillar eyebrows
hung like drapes above his eyes.

Smiling at the camera, the man then revealed the
sketch he'd just made—a squiggly-lined cartoon of two
boys who looked vaguely familiar.

"Hey," said Matt. "That looks like . . ."

"Us," Craz said, his mind struggling to figure out how

that could be even remotely possible. "That kid's even wearing my shirt."

"It's just a coincidence," said Matt. "Or a trick."

As if he had heard them, the man in the video flashed a toothy grin and then squished the cartoon into a ball before he chucked it off camera and gave his chair a big spin so that he went around and around like a little kid on a ride.

"Cartooning...is...fun!" he shouted, before stopping suddenly and looking directly at the boys. "Greetings," he began. "Boyd T. Boone here, and yup, if you're watching this, then you're probably already wondering if you want to cartoon with Boyd T. Boone. That answer better be, 'You betcha.' Otherwise you clicked on to the wrong place."

"Boyd T. Boone?" asked Matt. "Never heard of him."

"Of course you've probably never heard of me," the man in the video continued. "But that's no reason not to listen closely to what I have to offer."

"You heard the man," said Craz. "Let's hear what he's got to say."

Boyd T. Boone flashed his grin again. "I know what you want. You want to be taken seriously. You want to make people laugh. You want folks to stand up and notice your cartoons. Am I right?"

The boys both nodded.

Boyd T. Boone held up a mysterious purple satchel. "Well, then, just order my special one-of-a-kind cartooning kit, and I promise your world will never be the same." He dangled the purple pouch, letting it swing back and forth in his fingers.

"Cartooning kit! See, Matt? That's what I'm talking about! Told you we just needed the right supplies."

"Yeah, sure." Matt wasn't quite so positive. "What's the catch?"

"It's simple," Boyd T. Boone said as he walked close to the camera so that his face filled the screen. "Use my kit. Change your lives." Then he squished his caterpillar eyebrows together and got serious. "Order now before it's too late!"

The video ended, and the web page changed to a large blinking icon that simply read, *ORDER HERE*. A digital clock appeared beneath the words and began counting down from sixty seconds. Fifty-nine . . . fifty-eight . . . fifty-seven . . .

"Whoa. A time limit? Come on. Click it, Matt." Craz was sure that ordering the kit was the right thing to do. Who cared if the guy in the video was a little odd?

"No way," said Matt. "This is totally creepy." He reached for the mouse, wanting to click off the web page. "Besides, we don't even know what this is going to cost us."

Ding! The figure *$29.95* popped up on the screen.

"Thirty bucks?" Matt said. "That's way too much money."

Ding! A red *X* appeared over the *$29.95*. Next to it a flashing *$10* appeared. The countdown clock was down to thirty-six seconds.

"Ten bucks!" Craz said. "Even if all we get is a chewed-up pencil and a piece of an eraser, we can risk ten bucks."

Matt hesitated. "I don't know, man."

Craz got serious. "Come on. Aren't you sick and tired of no one knowing how good we are? And why is that? Because nobody gets a chance to ever see our stuff." Craz sighed. "If no one sees what we do, it's the same as not doing it."

"That's not true," said Matt. "I like to make cartoons for myself, not just so other kids see them."

"Fine. You keep filling your notebooks with stuff that no one's going to look at," Craz said. "But I'm telling you now, the only way to go from the kid in the back of the class who just doodles to the star cartoonist of the school is to get our stuff copied and out to other kids. We have to be seen to be noticed!"

The countdown clock on the screen was at fourteen seconds.

"I do want to be noticed," Matt said desperately. "It makes me sick that Diesel gets all the attention."

"You can draw circles around that little skunk."

"I know. His cartoons aren't even funny."

"Not like ours, my friend. That's why we need to take a chance. Five bucks each. That's all it takes."

The clock was at eight seconds, seven . . . six . . .

Craz grabbed the mouse and moved the cursor over the *ORDER* icon. "Well?" he asked. "Do it?"

The clock counted down. Four . . . three . . . two . . .

"Do it!" Matt shouted.

Craz clicked the mouse, and the ORDER button disappeared. Both guys let out a sigh of relief.

"See?" Craz said. "Taking chances is a good thing!"

Matt was about to agree, but then his whole computer came to a crashing halt. The screen went black. The power shut down. The hard drive gave off a sickening spinning sound.

"Oh, great," Matt moaned. "I bet we just downloaded a virus."

"You worry too much, Matt," Craz said. "If it's a virus, I can fix it. Look on the bright side. We took a chance. That's got to be a good thing."

Matt just shook his head. "Boyd T. Boone. What kind of a name is that?"

9
GYM

HATING MONDAYS WAS A NO-BRAINER. AND Tuesdays were no good because Craz and Matt had to sit through the painfully dull health class, where Mrs. Petrone, the teacher with the most peculiar overbite on earth, talked on and on about how adolescent boys' and girls' bodies change and grow like delicate flowers.

A typical Petrone-ism: "Showering often may reduce unwelcome body odors. Soap is your friend."

Soap is your friend? Try keeping a straight face listening to things like that!

But as terrible as Mrs. Petrone's Tuesday puberty PowerPoints were, Thursday was a much worse school day for the simple reason that Thursday was gym day.

"Let's go, Worfle," Coach Arakanian bellowed. "You can't hang up there all day." The wire-haired, bulky gym teacher shook his head in disgust while the rest of the class snickered and stared up at Matt, who hung helplessly on to the climbing rope that was suspended from the gym ceiling.

The problem? Matt was frozen in place. He'd somehow managed to pull himself halfway up the stupid rope, and now, thirty feet above his classmates, he clung fearfully to his lifeline, unable to move in either direction.

"You can do it, Matt," yelled Craz, trying to encourage his friend. "Use your upper body strength."

Matt knew he didn't have any upper body strength, or any body strength, for that matter. "Working on it!" he shouted back while looking down at the sea of expectant faces. He considered his options. The only thing between him and spending the rest of the school year on crutches was the gym mat, which was just two inches of compressed foam covered in blue vinyl. No way it would break his fall, and he doubted Jimbo Gilligan, the biggest kid in class, would catch him, though it did make a funny cartoon in his head.

While Matt hung on to the thick gym rope with every ounce of his energy, the jock kids started chanting, "Weak-ling! Weak-ling! Weak-ling!"

Coach Arakanian let the bullying continue. In his beady eyes the jocks at Kilgore could do no wrong, which left plenty of room for the muscle-impaired kids to be total flailing failures.

"Oh, man. I've got that nauseous thing going on again," Craz said, watching Matt sway helplessly from side to side.

"Tell me about it," said Sammy Kinsella, who, along

with Len Bruddle, stood behind the lean lineup of class-mates who were already placing bets on Matt's demise.

Matt felt like a cat trapped up in a tree. A big scaredy-cat.

Paulie Frick, the stuck-up quarterback for the Kilgore Killer Bees football team, grabbed hold of the other climbing rope. "I'll get him down, Coach. No sweat."

Effortlessly Paulie got into position—two hands above his head, feet clenched tightly below. Like a toy on a string he shot up the rope.

"Dude is like a spider monkey," Sammy Kinsella said through his retainer spit.

"See, this is where genetics pay off," added Len. "In my gene pool I can barely do the doggie paddle."

Matt closed his eyes. He hoped when he opened them that he would be back in bed and that this whole rope-climbing fiasco would be a really bad dream.

"Hey, dork," Paulie called out from the parallel rope. "I've seen six-year-old girls with more muscles than you."

"Gee, thanks, Paulie," Matt said from his position dangling above the class. "Way to boost my confidence."

"Like I really care about your confidence or whether you break every bone in your pathetic body. I'm just up here as eye candy for *las chicas*."

Sure enough, Paulie hung on to his rope with one hand and was flexing his muscles in the hopes that the girls' class in the other half of the gym would notice him. Matt looked past Paulie and his muscles to where the seventh-grade girls were busy playing badminton.

Paulie Frick whistled through his teeth so that the girls would check him out, which of course they did. Donna Gerland waved her badminton racket, and Patty Lintoff showed off with a handstand.

Matt closed his eyes tightly, hoping he could be invisible.

"Hey, Romeo," Paulie said. "Wave to the ladies."

Matt looked again. Most of the girls were laughing and pointing at him. Matt wanted to die, which, given his precarious situation, was a distinct possibility.

The only good news for Matt was that Cindy Ockabloom was too busy lacing her sneakers to look up. Even from this distance Matt could see just how pretty she looked in the saggy gray gym uniform.

MATT Sez:

Drawing is FASTER than WORKING OUT!

Her honey-brown hair was tied back in a ponytail, and Matt could almost picture that one cute freckle on the back of her neck—the one he'd stared at all year, sitting at the desk behind her during sixth grade. Matt wished he was more like Paulie and could get girls to like him just by showing up. But Matt wasn't the kid with the muscles and perfect smile. Sure, he could draw stuff like that, but he'd never *be* that kind of guy.

Paulie waved once more to the girls, then turned to Matt and hissed, "Listen, you're going to climb down the dumb rope and get your sorry butt onto that gym mat. Got it?"

Matt took a deep breath and then clenched his knees tightly against the rough rope before starting his slow slide down.

"That's gotta hurt," Sammy slurred.

"No doubt," Craz said, already worried his best friend

might have a hard time drawing new cartoons anytime soon.

After he was safely on the ground and Paulie was off getting high fives from the other football players, Matt plopped down, exhausted and red-faced, onto the gym bleachers, wishing the bell would just hurry up and ring.

"Okay, leeches," Coach Arakanian bellowed to the class. "Fifty laps. Move it!"

All Matt could do was moan.

10

THE PACKAGE

MATT GOT OFF THE BUS AND WALKED TOWARD his house, hoping to forget the school day completely. He just wanted to grab something to eat, head to his room, and get lost in drawing. Doodling always made him feel better, which is why he knew filling a blank page with nonsense would help erase the day he'd just had.

Ricky sat alone on the couch, watching TV with his dirty sneakers propped up on the coffee table. A carton of mocha chip ice cream sat dripping on the couch cushions, and an electric guitar lay across the canyon of his lap.

"Hey, runt," Ricky grunted without looking away from his favorite program. It was a rerun of one of those cop shows where the cameras follow police around as they try to catch some deadbeat thief. Ricky couldn't get enough of that reality stuff. "Dad called. Guess what? No visit this weekend. Something about a thing at work. Deadlines. Working late. The usual stuff. I don't even listen anymore."

Matt nodded. This was the third weekend in a row that his dad had to cancel. Since he'd moved out of the house three months ago the weekend stays at his

condo had been getting less frequent and his excuses lamer. Before he'd separated from Matt's mom, it hadn't mattered as much that work was so important. His clothes had been hanging in the closet. His dirty dishes had been in the sink. Parts of him had been home even when he wasn't. But now? Even though he only lived on the other side of town, it felt like he was gone for good.

"So where'd the guitar come from? You know what Mom said."

"Borrowed it from Foomer. And what Mom doesn't know won't kill you. Got it?"

Matt knew Ricky had been after his parents for the past year to get him a guitar. He'd practically gotten on his knees and begged for one. His parents had even gotten into a big fight about it. His dad had instantly said yes. But his mom thought Ricky should bring his grades up before he got something that would be even more of a distraction from his schoolwork. Of course Ricky's grades never moved out of the toilet, and even though that didn't stop his begging, he'd been forbidden to get the guitar.

"And Mom hates when you put your sneakers on the table." Matt instantly wished he hadn't said that. Why did he care what Ricky did?

"Good thing she's not home yet, isn't it?" Ricky glared back at Matt through the slits of his eyes. If looks could kill, then Matt would have been six feet under. Ricky dug deep into the ice cream carton without taking his eyes off his younger brother, then shoved a mega-spoonful into his mouth.

Matt really missed having a brother who was his friend.

"Oh, yeah. Mail came for you." Ricky pointed toward the hall with the spoon, which dripped ice cream all over the back of the couch. "I put it in your room. You can thank me later."

Mail? Matt never got mail unless it was a birthday card from his grandparents or an overdue notice from the library. He dropped his backpack onto the edge of the couch and headed down the hallway, curious to see what was waiting for him inside his room.

"LARRY! TELL MEAGAN TO MOVE HER BARBIE. She's ruining my zoo!"

"Am not!"

"Are too!"

"*Am not!*"

Craz's head hurt. Becca, his older sister, had band practice, and his older brother, Hank, was at his after-school job at the Shack, which meant Craz was stuck babysitting Meagan and Pete. According to his parents, getting to take care of his younger siblings was the bonus part of turning thirteen.

Really? He'd been thirteen for three months, and so far becoming an actual teenager had only gotten him

more chores around the house and a puny fifty-cent raise in allowance. The "bonus" part seemed pretty much a no-show.

"Get that rhinoceros off of me," Meagan whined. "Lar-ry! Pete's hurting my arm!"

"Fine!" Craz's little brother let go of the rhino, then grabbed the Barbie doll by her ponytail and dangled it over his toy crocodile. "But in a real zoo Barbie would get eaten by crocodiles."

Meagan snarled. "In a real zoo crocodiles wouldn't be missing a leg." She grabbed the toy croc and yanked on its stubby plastic leg until it popped out from the body.

"Nooooooo!" Pete screamed, then jumped at his sister with flailing arms. "Give. It. Back!"

Craz sighed loudly, wishing for the hundredth time that he was an only child.

"All right, you guys. That's it," he said, pulling his brother and sister apart before one of them went total commando. It was bad enough that he had to take care of these two. He didn't need to get in trouble for letting them hurt each other.

The phone rang, and Craz did what any great baby-sitter would do. He turned on the TV and told his sister and brother to watch cartoons. Disaster averted.

He reached for the hallway phone. "Hello? Insane asylum."

"Craz, you're not going to believe this," Matt said excitedly. "But it's here."

Craz sat back on the carpeted stairway, where he could still keep an eye on his sister and brother, who sat safely glued to the television. "What are you talking about, Matt?"

Matt paced his room staring at the unopened box on his bed. "The cartooning kit. From online . . ."

Craz laughed. "Dude, we never even gave them your name or address or anything. The computer crashed. Remember?"

Matt reached for the shoe-box-size package. "Look, I don't know how it got here—but it did."

Craz was about to tell Matt that he was nuts, when he heard the unmistakable sound of something smashing to the floor. One quick look at the guilty faces of his little brother and sister told the story. "Gotta go. Text me," was all he said before hanging up.

MATT PUT THE PHONE DOWN AND INSPECTED the package. The postmark was a blurry, unreadable mess, and the only actual writing on it was his name and address, which had been scribbled sloppily with a dark blue pen. But Craz was right. They'd never filled out an address or given any name. How did that Internet site know who Matt was and where he lived?

Matt put the box on his desk and sat on his bed, trying to decide if he should open it or not. Five seconds later he was on his feet. Of course he'd see what was inside!

Using the letter opener that had been his dad's, Matt slit the box open and peeled back the cardboard flaps. The first thing he saw was a layer of packing peanuts. When he was a kid, he'd had a fantasy of filling a swimming pool with these things and then jumping in. He still thought that would be a blast even if he knew he'd never really do it.

Digging around in the box, Matt was surprised to find a soft velvet pouch, which he lifted out from the sea of peanuts.

The purple satchel was just like the one the weird guy in the video had held. Matt turned the bag over, feeling the weight of whatever was inside and letting the plush velvet brush against his fingertips. He imagined rubbing the soft bag against his face, but then felt stupid about it.

Matt reached for the slipknot, loosened the string, and then tipped the bag over onto his desk. Out came a medium-size glass bottle of black ink and a dark leather oblong box with a small clasp that kept it tightly shut.

First Matt lifted the rectangular box, being careful to open it slowly.

"Whoa," he said as he stared at a beautiful pen, which was a shade of green so deep it was almost blue. With its intricate silver designs that went up and down the length of the tapered pen shaft, Matt guessed it had to be an antique. Unscrewing the cap revealed the pen point. It was unlike any pen Matt had ever used. Instead of a simple tip like on one of his crummy ballpoint pens, this pen used a special drawing nib, which was a thin diamond-shaped silver extension that looked just like the beak of a small bird.

He unscrewed the shaft of the pen, which easily slid off to reveal an empty clear plastic tube that connected to the pen nib.

"I guess that's where the ink goes," Matt said, glancing at the bottle of black ink on his desk.

Matt screwed the shaft back on and then gripped the pen between his thumb and forefinger. Instantly the pen made him feel special, like a real cartoonist. "Smooth," he said, imagining how cool he'd look doodling with the ornate pen. "No more cheapo plastic pens for me!"

He set the pen back in its case and then picked up the ink, which came in a pyramid-shaped glass bottle with a cork stopper on top. Matt held the bottle up to the lamp, but the dark liquid was so thick, no light shone through. Matt shook the bottle and then watched the inky mass swirl like a tornado of darkness inside the glass.

He held the ink in one hand and the new pen in the other. Obviously the ink needed to go inside the pen. That's how it works. Matt had never thought about the connection between a pen and its ink before. Pens were just the things you used to make lines, and the lines made shapes, and those shapes became his cartoons. But this kit kept the pen separated from the ink. For the first time Matt thought about how you can't have one without the other. A bottle of ink won't do you any good without a pen—and a pen without ink might look cool, but it isn't going to draw anything.

HONK! HONK! The car horn startled him. That would be his mom. She only honked twice when she needed help unloading groceries. Fine. Let Ricky help her, he thought.

"Hey, egghead. Go help Mom," Ricky shouted from the living room.

"You help her!" Matt screamed back. "I'm busy."

"Well, I'm older," he bellowed.

The double horn blasts repeated, shorter this time, which meant his mom was getting impatient out in the driveway.

"Do it, Matt. Now!" Ricky yelled.

Matt sighed and then put the pen and ink back into the purple satchel. He'd have to wait to try his new cartooning supplies but was already imagining how they were going to make a difference in his comics.

A huge difference.

11

PEN + INK = AWESOME!

"YOU JUST CAME HOME FROM THE SUPERMARKET," Ricky complained as he crumpled potato chips onto the steaming plate in front of him and then shoveled a bite into his mouth. "Tonight's supposed to be something good."

"Do we have to go through this every week, Ricky? First we use up last week's food, and *then* we eat the new stuff," Matt's mom said. "Besides, it's Thursday. Tuna Noodle Casserole night. Right, Matt?"

Matt felt his brother's kick under the table but just smiled back at his mom. "Yup. You don't mess with Tuna Noodle Casserole night."

"I'd sure like to mess with *you*," Ricky muttered.

Matt usually took Ricky's bait and ended up in an insult slugfest with him, which always lead to his mother's screaming for them to both grow up, before excusing herself from the table and slamming her bedroom door.

But tonight Matt let Ricky's put-down roll off his back. He just wanted dinner over with so he could retreat to his room and start using his new pen and ink. That's why he skipped dessert, and instead of a ten-minute argument over who would do the dishes, he simply got up to do them himself. Right away.

Ricky left the house to go study at Foomer's, which meant he was really going to hang out behind the 7-Eleven and try to meet girls.

While Matt dried the dishes, his mom disappeared into the family room to read the newspaper, which she always did with the TV on, as if having one of those dull CNN news guys blabber in the background was the same as having someone to talk to. At least it filled the house with noise that wasn't what he'd grown used to—his parents' fighting.

Finally Matt was back in his room, staring at the

fancy pen and bottle of ink
that now lay beside the empty
purple satchel.

First things first: Matt
carefully filled the pen's
cartridge using the black ink, which was so dark and
dense, he could almost see his reflection in it.

Once the pen was full of ink, he pulled a clean sheet
of paper out from his desk drawer. "Here goes nothing,"
he said as he lifted the pen up like a saber he imagined
could cut down an army of skeletons. Or draw them,
anyway.

Whoosh. The first line just slid out from the pen tip.
It was like skating on a perfectly smooth sheet of ice, he
thought as the pen just glided across the white paper,
leaving a thick, wet line behind.

Matt spent the next hour getting used to his new
pen.

After filling several sheets with practice sketches,
Matt drew one of his old standby characters, a ten-ton
ninja potato, who just happened to be a hundred feet tall.

Spudzilla looked killer, Matt thought, proud of the

cartoon that stared back at him with its dark black eyes. He let his mind wander, imagining how cool it was going to be to finally have his cartoons seen, and not just by Craz but by kids at school and people on the bus and strangers who might see one of his cartoons and say, "Now that's a funny comic."

And what about Cindy? What would it feel like to know she was admiring his cartoons? Maybe his cartoons would actually help him talk to her.

He looked again at his new cartooning supplies. That Boyd guy was right. Matt was ready to take his cartooning to the next level. And for the first time in a long time, he felt like his dream was possible—to one day be a famous cartoonist and actually make money from drawing comics.

An idea popped into his head, and he was so excited by it that he grabbed a fresh sheet of paper and drew the comic right away.

It took two hours and several tries to get it right. But Matt was finally happy with the way the cartoon turned out. Placing the cap back onto the fancy pen, he leaned back in his chair and admired the new comic.

"Cartoon Kings," he said aloud. "That's what we're going to be." And then he lifted the pen into the air and drew an invisible crown above his head and sighed, "Cartoon Kings."

12

OFF LIMITS

"DUDE, THAT'S A CRAZY COMIC." CRAZ WAS LOOKING
over Matt's "Cartoon Kings" for the fifth time in twenty
minutes.

"The lines are pretty sweet, aren't they?" Matt pulled
the new pen from his shirt pocket and admired it again.
"This sucker really knows how to draw."

Third period was their study period, and both boys
had gotten library slips so they could quietly brainstorm some new comic ideas. They sat at the round
table by the back stacks across from a table of giggling
girls busy taking a boy-crush quiz inside some glossy
magazine.

"You know what, amigo?" Craz said, holding up the

new cartoon. "This comic is going to kick butt. I say we take it right to Turkle."

"Hold on," said Matt. "No more originals. I can't watch him destroy another cartoon."

"Good call," said Craz. "Let's make a few copies of this masterpiece."

Matt beamed. He never got tired of hearing Craz rave about his artwork. "Okay. We can swing by Copy-Copy after school."

"Nah," Craz said. "Why spend cash when we can do it for free here at school?"

Matt looked at his friend. "Craz, you know students can't use the school copy machines."

"Correction. We can't *get caught* using the school copy machines." Craz grinned.

Matt slumped a little lower in his chair. It was clear that Craz had a plan that Matt knew he was about to go along with.

MATT KEPT WATCH IN THE HALLWAY WHILE CRAZ opened the door to the empty teachers' lounge and slipped inside unseen. They'd both gotten bathroom passes from

the librarian, Ms. Gallaro, and had left the library minutes apart.

Kids were always talking about the mysterious room
where teachers disappeared in between classes, but
Craz had never actually seen the place up close. Sure,
he'd peeked in through the smudged door window and
glimpsed his teachers laughing and drinking coffee. But
it had always been just a passing glance, like he was looking in at the animals in a zoo.

Now that he was on the inside, he saw the truth:
Teachers were pigs. Crumpled newspapers, mismatched
furniture, a grease-stained doughnut box that still had
a half-eaten chocolate-covered and two jelly doughnuts

inside. And there was the tiny sink swollen full of dirty coffee cups and ancient, mold-covered plates that looked like they were science experiments gone horribly wrong.

"And I thought I was a slob," Craz said as he moved away from the awful sink stink and walked toward the Holy Grail of his quest: the teachers' copy machine.

Back in the hallway Matt paced nervously, hoping Craz would just hurry up and get this over with. He wasn't good at being on lookout. He was antsy and nervous, and his mind always thought about the worst-case scenarios, which in this case meant he was already picturing getting caught and landing a month-long detention . . . at least!

Craz went over to the counter and grabbed one of the jelly doughnuts and shoved it into his mouth. He grabbed a second one and held it up to see if Matt wanted a dough- nut too, but Matt just rolled his eyes and shook his head. "Whatever," Craz said as he stuffed the extra doughnut into his back pocket and then walked to the cramped alcove where the copier sat. This was it. Mission accom- plished.

Craz looked over his shoulder at the door, and Matt quickly gave him the thumbs-up sign. The coast was clear.

Perfect. Craz pulled the "Cartoon Kings" comic out from beneath his T-shirt and was glad he hadn't ruined it with any of his body sweat, though he did give it a quick whiff to make sure it hadn't absorbed any unwanted smells. "Stink-free," he said, and then lifted the copier cover and placed the drawing down on the glass.

Back in the hall Matt was a wreck. He was chewing on his thumbnail when all of a sudden his English teacher, Mrs. Bentz, rounded the hallway corner and waddled straight toward the teachers' lounge. Lucky for him, she was busy pulling down student council campaign posters that Jake Greenberg had plastered on every classroom door and empty wall space. The vote had been last Monday, and Jake had gotten a total of eight votes, which was pretty lame.

"'Vote Green'? I think not." Mrs. Bentz snorted as the stack of bright handmade posters grew in her clutches. She was glad he hadn't won. Based on an unfortunate episode involving a rubber band and several well-aimed paper clips, she did not think that Jake Greenberg was student council president material.

Matt's first instinct was to run—but he remembered

the plan and gave Craz the warning signal—three quick knocks on the door.

And then he ran.

Craz had finally made all the correct settings on the copier, when he heard the warning signal, and he froze in place. He had to make a choice—copy the cartoon and risk getting caught, or quickly hide. Though he was seconds away from success, he decided to play it safe and slid behind the ratty couch by the window, leaving the cartoon still under the lid of the copy machine.

Mrs. Bentz opened the teachers' lounge door with an armload of posters, which she easily dropped into the recycle bin. "Bye-bye, Mr. Greenberg."

Though he couldn't see who it was, Craz knew from her voice that his awful English teacher had just walked in, and he quickly ducked lower behind the couch.

Sploosh! He felt the jelly from the doughnut in his back pocket ooze out onto his pants, instantly reminding him that his pocket was a dumb place to put a doughnut, jelly or any other kind. He pictured the gooey mess on his butt and knew that was the least of his problems.

From his hiding spot Craz could see Mrs. Bentz's

thick ankles and ugly black shoes as she walked past the couch and then out of sight.

He didn't dare take another peek. Instead he sat listening for clues, wondering what Mrs. Bentz was doing. The clinking of coffee cups told Craz that she was probably pouring herself a cup of the brown sludge that he imagined had been sitting in the coffeepot all morning.

After a long moment of silence, he suddenly felt the couch shift under her weight. She was right on top of him! Looking up, he could see her gray-streaked hair that was always pulled into a tight bun. His nostrils filled with her sick perfume that reminded him of the ocean . . . at low tide. He almost gagged on the stench.

The couch shook again as Mrs. Bentz settled into the soft cushions. "Ah, now that's cozy," she said to no one.

Craz was trapped, but he peered slowly around the arm of the couch and could see the copier just fifteen feet away. If only he could get rid of her, he thought. At least he felt safe in his hiding place. As long as she just sat there, he'd be okay. Unless . . .

Fffft.

Did his English teacher really just let a ripe one rip? Oh, man—it was foul. It combined with the gross smell of her perfume, and Craz had to do everything in his power not to puke.

Meanwhile, Matt was hiding in the boys' bathroom, feeling helpless and just a little silly that he'd run away. Pacing back and forth in front of the row of sinks, he tried to come up with a plan to rescue Craz. After all, wasn't that exactly what Craz would do for him? He had to come up with a way to get Mrs. Bentz out of the teachers' lounge and do it before the bell rang and the hallway filled back up with students and worse—teachers on their way to the lounge.

Matt checked his watch. 11:20. He still had five minutes. Plenty of time, if he'd had half a clue what to do next.

Craz wasn't sure how much longer he could stand being surrounded by all of Mrs. Bentz's odd odors, and just as he was deciding to simply stand up, say hello, and then bolt out the door and into some breathable air, there was a repeated loud knock at the door.

Mrs. Bentz rose up from the couch. "Hold your horses. I'm coming."

Finally breathing again, Craz peeked around the couch and watched his English teacher open the door. He couldn't believe who was standing there.

"H-hello, Mrs. Bentz," Matt stammered. "I was wondering if I could ask you a question?"

Mrs. Bentz wrinkled her nose into an uncomfortable shape. "Come see me during class time, Matthew."

She started closing the door. Matt had to act fast, and so he took the surest shot he could. "It's about *Treasure Island*, ma'am. And the symbolism of the one-legged Long John Silver."

Students never wanted to discuss her favorite book, and so Mrs. Bentz smiled and opened the door wide. "*Treasure Island*! How wonderful!" she exclaimed. "Come in, Matthew. Come in."

Oh, no, Matt thought. He wanted to get her *out* of the room, not be invited to come *in*. Thinking fast, Matt said,

"Would it be too much trouble if we go to my locker first? All my notes are there. I hope."

Faster than you could say "Jim Hawkins," Mrs. Bentz was out the teachers' lounge door and walking side by side with Matt, lecturing him on the merits of Robert Louis Stevenson's prose. Matt did his best to pretend to listen, but really he was just hoping Craz could now escape unseen.

Craz was impressed with Matt's quick thinking. He stood up and took a deep breath, then ran to the copy machine and hit the green button. The machine hummed for a second, and then the bright light flashed from under the glass. Normally that would have been it—the copy would have been made. But something different happened. As soon as the original had been copied, a second flash of light filled the room, this one even brighter, so bright that Craz had to cover his eyes with his hand.

"What was that?" Craz asked as the copy of the cartoon was finally spit from the machine.

The bell rang, and Craz realized he had to get out of the teachers' lounge before he got caught. If he timed it right, he could just melt into the sea of hallway kids

before any of the teachers came
into the room.

He stood by the door and
waited until the hallway was
full, and then simply opened
the door and walked away with the copy of Matt's cartoon
in his hands.

Piece of cake, Craz thought, totally forgetting that
he had nearly suffocated on Mrs. Bentz's body odor . . .
and that he'd left the original cartoon inside the copy
machine.

13

LOCKER SURPRISE

CRAZ WAS IN LINE FOR A HOT LUNCH, WHILE
Matt sat at their usual table, which was wedged in
between the overflowing garbage cans and the air-
conditioning unit that always dripped.

Matt's Friday "sandwich surprise" lay mysteriously
wrapped in front of him, but for once he didn't care what
was for lunch. He was too busy staring off at Cindy
Ockabloom, who was wearing a perfect gold and blue
skirt and a yellow top the color of ripe bananas. She
sat, as she always did, at the "Middles" table, located (of
course) in the center of the lunch table universe. The
Middles were kids who weren't popular. They weren't
losers. They were just kids who got decent grades, didn't

play sports, and never wound up in detention or stuck washing teachers' cars as punishment for wasting valuable classroom time.

Len Bruddle sat down next to Matt and Sammy Kinsella. He immediately recognized the far-off look in his friend's face. "Cindy?"

Matt didn't blink. "Cindy."

"Dude, just go up and say hi to her. The suspense is killing you."

Matt snapped out of his trance and turned to his friends. "It's not that easy, Len. Look at her. She's perfect."

Sammy removed his retainer so he could eat his lunch. Bologna and yellow mustard on rye bread—no crusts. "She's not perfect, Matt. I sit behind her in Spanish class.

She picks her fingernails and then smells her fingers."

"Smells them? No way!" Matt pictured Cindy and her stinky nails. He sighed. "That's so cute."

Sammy shook his head and took a bite from his sandwich. "Cute? Really? We definitely have different definitions."

Matt sighed. "She's just so . . . so . . ."

"Out of your galaxy?" Len smiled. "Look, Matt, you've really got nothing to lose. She already doesn't talk to you. It can't get any worse."

Matt looked over at Cindy's table. She was laughing hysterically at something Gretchen Gosling had said. *Amazing,* Matt thought. *She looks great even with milk spurting out of her nose. Maybe Len is right. Just go say hi. Break the ice. Maybe even crack a little joke.*

"You really think I should?" Matt asked.

"Definitely," said Len. "You'll thank me later. Trust me."

Matt took a deep breath and then pushed his chair away from the lunch table. Defiant, he was going to walk over to Cindy's table and act as casually as his nervous system would allow. *No problemo,* he told himself as he crossed the cafeteria with butterflies in his stomach.

* * *

THE LUNCH LINE MOVED AT A TURTLE'S PACE,
and hungry kids were getting impatient. Craz didn't really
care. He was busy staring at the "Cartoon Kings" comic
that he'd successfully copied in the teachers' lounge. He
couldn't put his finger on it, but there was something
really different about this cartoon. It had Matt's loose
line style, but there was something else going on in the
drawing. Something he couldn't quite describe. Maybe
that new pen really was making a difference.

"What's the holdup?" shouted Paulie Frick, who wasn't
used to waiting for anything. "Come on, speed it up!"

Bobby "Bruno" Brunell, the barrel-shaped linebacker
for the Killer Bees, mimicked Paulie and pounded his fist
against the wall. "Yeah, speed it up. I'm hungry!"

The two football players pushed past kids and easily
cut their way through the long line. It was the junior high
pecking order that placed jocks above mere mortals, and
so Craz just stood in line and watched as smaller kids got
knocked against the wall and reshuffled like cards.

Craz finally arrived at the hot food station run by
Mrs. Murtha, the lunch lady with the nickel-size mole

on her chin who had the best spoon control in the cafeteria. Mrs. Murtha could scoop out a helping of peas and then drop a perfect dab of mashed potatoes dead center onto your plate with her eyes closed.

"Next!" she called out, her one lazy eye pointing just slightly off to the left.

Craz slid his plate beneath her heaping spoon and watched as an ice cream scoop of macaroni and hamburger fell with a loud *Splat.*

The food looked inedible, which didn't really bother Craz. "And toss in a chocolate milk," he said to the cashier, knowing a carton of the chocolate drink would wash down even the worst that the cafeteria had to dish out.

"Two-fifty," the cashier said.

Craz was busy scoping out the cafeteria scene and so he wasn't looking at the cashier. He automatically held out his money as he spotted Matt making his move over at Cindy's table. "Way to go, buddy," Craz said a second before Paulie Frick and Bruno tripped Matt, who bumped into Gary McMillan, whose lunch tray shot through the air, spilling mashed potatoes, meatballs, and grape juice all over Cindy Ockabloom.

The whole cafeteria erupted in applause and hoots and hollers. Craz cringed as he watched Matt stand helplessly in front of food-covered Cindy.

"Here's your change," the cashier said as two coins dropped into Craz's open palm. "By the way, tell your friend nothing removes grape juice stains like baking soda, seltzer water, and a little elbow grease."

Craz now looked at the cashier and just stared with his mouth hanging open. Instead of the usual cashier, who looked like his grandmother and smelled like a dog, this new cashier was the spitting image of Boyd T. Boone, the cartoonist from the Internet who'd sold him and Matt the cartooning supplies.

Of course, this version of the cartoonist wore a

white dress-smock, black knee socks, and a hairnet—but, come on. Look at that mustache! Craz was positive it was the strange dude from the website.

"Oh, and if you ask me, chocolate milk is the nectar of the gods," the cashier said, and then winked at Craz, who finally picked up his tray and slowly walked off to join his friends.

"That was weird," Craz said as he looked back over his shoulder and was even more dismayed to see that Boyd T. Boone was no longer there. The cashier was her usual old-lady self again.

"O-kay," Craz said as he decided to keep to himself what he'd just seen. "No more four-cupcake breakfasts for me."

THE SCHOOL DAY WAS FINALLY OVER, AND MATT was on his way to his locker when Craz caught up to him.

"There he is. Mr. Smooth."

Even though it had been a few hours, the memory of his lunchroom spill was still too fresh. Matt was in no mood for any of Craz's jokes.

"Can we just drop it?" Matt hoped he wouldn't have to see Cindy again. Not today. Not ever.

"Absolutely," said Craz. "I'm just saying there are other ways to get a girl to like you. You don't have to ruin her clothes. I'm pretty sure that's the opposite of what works."

Matt shook his head. Why had he listened to Len and tried to have an actual conversation with her? He was perfectly happy keeping his crush a one-way street that only he knew about.

"Like you're the expert, huh, Craz?" Matt said. "The only girls you actually talk to are the ones who tell you to keep a five-foot radius from them."

"True that, my friend. I do seem to have a toxic effect on the ladies."

"It's not easy being us," Matt sighed.

"Nope," added Craz as he threw a friendly arm around Matt's shoulder. "But at least we got each other."

They walked down the crowded hall and stopped by Matt's locker.

"So, gonna take your new cartoon pen out for another test drive?" Craz asked. "Your 'Cartoon Kings' comic was pretty great."

Matt took the new pen out of his shirt pocket and again admired how cool it looked. "Yeah, I plan on starting a new 'Cyclops Cops' comic when I get home. Got to fill up the pen with ink first, but then, doodle madness!" Matt put the pen away and then fumbled with his locker combination. "I'm really glad you suggested we get some good supplies. This new pen does make me feel like a real cartoonist."

Matt opened his locker, and both boys gasped.

Sitting on the bottom of the locker was a cloth bag with a large dollar sign scribbled on the side. Craz reached down and pulled on the bag. It was heavy.

Matt was so shocked, he could barely talk. "You know what it looks like, don't you?"

Craz reached into his backpack and whipped out the copy of Matt's "Cartoon Kings" cartoon. Sure enough, the bag in the locker looked just like the bag

of money that Matt had drawn.

"But how—" Matt started to ask, but Craz cut him off.

"Forget how." Craz opened the bag. Both boys peered inside and saw that it was full of dollar bills. "*How much? That's the question!*"

"Is it real?" Matt reached into the bag and pulled out one of the bills. He held it up to the light. He rubbed it between his fingers. He even crumpled it up and then smoothed it back flat. "It sure looks real."

"There's only one way to find out," Craz said as he stuffed his pockets with cash. "Let's go spend it!"

"I don't know, Craz. Maybe it's not really ours."

Craz put a hand on his friend's shoulder. "Live a little,

okay? You drew a cartoon where a bag of money shows up in your locker. I don't know how this happened, but wouldn't you rather spend now and ask questions later?"

Matt looked at the cartoon again. The money bag in his locker did look exactly like the one in his cartoon.

"Besides," Craz added, "I sure could go for something to eat. What do you say, buddy?" He pulled a handful of bills from his pocket and waved them in Matt's face. "My treat!"

14

THE SHACK

THE SHACK WAS *THE* AFTER-SCHOOL HANGOUT
place. Crammed between the Bran & Tan natural-food
store and the town post office, the cozy burger joint
was decorated like a rock-and-roll diner, with red vinyl
booths, and jukeboxes at every table. Junior high and
high school kids liked to stop by on their way home and
grab an ice cream or orders of fries. It was a spot popular
kids liked to go to, which made it pretty much off-limits
to Craz and Matt.

"Oh, man. We are *so* gonna buy stuff with this loot!"
Craz jammed a fistful of french fries into his mouth. His
other hand rested on his backpack, where the bag full of

money was safely hidden. "I'm guessing there's, like, a hundred bucks in there. At least!"

Matt was too confused to eat anything, which hadn't stopped Craz from ordering everything. French fries, cheeseburgers, two milk shakes, one order of onion rings, and a couple of Shack brownie super sundaes with extra hot fudge were scattered around the table, as if a junk food bomb had just exploded.

HANK—
the most BORING boy in the WORLD!

Craz's older brother, Hank, was working his busboy/waiter/dishwasher job, and when he saw the huge amount of food that Craz had ordered, he got all detective on him.

"Where'd you get that much money, Larry?" Hank asked as he cleaned a pile of dirty dishes from the booth behind them.

"None of your business, that's where," Craz shot back. "And bring us a couple of ice cream sodas. Big ones."

"You'll spoil your appetite for dinner, you know."

Craz rolled his eyes. "We both know Mom's cooking is inedible. Might as well fill up now while the getting is good."

Hank scribbled the order on his notepad and trudged off, leaving Craz to shake his head. "My brother is such a lump of mud!"

Matt looked at the "Cartoon Kings" comic again. "It just doesn't make any sense."

"Look, it doesn't really matter *how* this happened," Craz said between bites of his cheeseburger. "Isn't it enough that it *did* happen?"

"But I don't believe in magic," Matt said. "There's got to be some other explanation."

"I dunno, man. You draw a cartoon where there's a bag of money in your locker, and the next thing you know, there's a bag of money in your locker. Sounds pretty magical to me!"

Craz grabbed his milk shake and took a long swig, which left a strawberry stripe above his lip. "This is the greatest day ever!"

"And you're sure the money is real? I mean, this isn't

some lame joke that Diesel and Skip pulled, right?"

Craz eased his hand into the money sack and pulled out a wad of dollar bills. "Do these look like fake bucks to you?"

Matt had to admit the facts: The money looked real, and only an idiot would give away a bag full of real money as a practical joke. Besides, Craz's logic might have been weird, but it did *sort of* make sense. Matt had used the new pen to draw a cartoon where money was in his locker. Could that really be the answer?

"Two ice cream sodas," Hank said as he placed the tall glasses on the already crowded table. "And I'm still wondering how you plan on paying for all this."

Craz looked at his older brother. Hank was sixteen years old but seemed like an old man. He was the annoying kind of kid who always did the right thing. When he was failing a subject, he hired his own tutor. When he broke a window with a baseball, he fixed it himself. He was responsible, which explained why he had this lousy job at the Shack, a job most kids would hate and do only because they had to. But Hank loved the work and came home after every shift boasting about what a great opportunity the cruddy job was.

"Don't worry, Hank," Craz began. "We've got the cash, so be a good man and just buzz off."

Hank put his hands on his hips and stared down at his younger brother. He put on his disapproving "Dad voice" and said, "You better not be doing anything I wouldn't do. You hear me, Larry?"

Craz laughed. "When did you stop being a kid? Here." Craz stuffed the wad of dollar bills into the pocket of Hank's stained apron. "Go buy yourself something nice. Now scram!"

Hank looked at the crumpled bills, shook his head, and walked back toward the kitchen.

"Listen, Craz," Matt said, "maybe you want to go easy on that cash."

"I don't see why," Craz said as he started to fold a dollar bill into a small paper airplane. "If we run out, all you have to do is draw more."

Craz flashed a goofy grin at Matt and then sailed the dollar airplane off across the diner. It landed right in front of Marci Baer, a pretty girl in eighth grade, who shrieked at the sudden sight of a free dollar.

"We don't know that's how it works," cautioned Matt. "Not for sure."

Craz leaned across the skyline of food on the table. "Then, let's find out. You've got the pen, right?"

Matt slowly smiled. Sure, why not try it again? If it worked, great. And if it didn't? There was no harm in testing the idea. "Okay," he said. "Let's see if it's because of the pen."

Matt pulled the pen from his pocket and cleared the french-fry plate and ice cream soda glass off his place mat. He smoothed the paper down as if he was petting a soft cat. "What should I draw?"

Craz knew instantly. "A forty-foot tall school-crushing robot-a-saurus!"

"Craz. I'm serious."

"And you think I'm kidding?"

At that instant Hank came over to the table. He was practically hyperventilating, and his eyeballs were bulging out of his pinched face. "Do you realize you gave me eighteen dollars? Larry, eighteen dollars? Something is wrong here. Why do you have all this money to just toss around?"

"Don't you have dishes to wash?" Craz fumed. "I told you, Hank. It's. None. Of. Your. Business."

Hank shook his head. "You worry me, Larry. I'm going to have to tell Mother and Father."

The ding from the kitchen window meant someone's order was ready, and Hank shook his head one more time and then rushed over to load up his tray.

As soon as Hank was gone, Craz knew what Matt should draw. "Make my brother into a geezer."

"What?"

"A geezer. An old man. You heard him. 'Tell *Mother* and *Father*.' Who says stuff like that? My brother acts like he's a hundred—let's make him that way."

Matt glanced across the diner and watched Hank precariously carry a tray of burgers over to a booth of kids. Matt studied his posture and then summed up his face—small hook of a nose, eyes too close together, curly scrub-brush hair, and ears that looked like folded potato chips.

"Sure. Why not? 'Old Man Hank.' Here goes nothing."

Matt wasn't sure what was going to happen as he clenched the pen between his fingers. He hesitated for a moment, unsure if he should even try, and then he took a deep breath and started to draw on the food-stained place mat.

15

BEE CAREFUL

"IS THAT IT?" CRAZ ASKED.

"I guess so," said Matt as he turned the sketch around for Craz to see. "I mean, it's not my best work, but I think it looks like Hank if he was, like, fifty years older."

The guys looked across the room and watched sixteen-year-old Hank lug a heavy tub of dirty dishes through the swinging doors and into the kitchen.

"What happens next?" Craz asked.

"Hey, I'm just as clueless as you. Maybe—"

CRASH! Plates and glasses smashed to the floor, and a second later Mr. Nuss, the owner and short-order cook of the diner, screamed, "Hank!"

A table of older kids was already hooting and clapping at the mishap.

"It worked!" Craz shouted. "The pen made Hank an old dude who can't carry stuff!"

Matt stared at the pen. This was all too strange. "I can't believe it. All I did was draw."

"All you did was *awesome*!" Craz said. "Unbelievably awesome!"

Matt lifted up the cartoon of Hank as an old man, and then raised his ice cream soda glass. "To the pen!"

"To the pen," said Craz as he clinked sodas with Matt and then took a huge sip of his drink. He burped, then started laughing. "We did it. My older brother is really old!"

The guys stared at the kitchen door in anticipation of geezer Hank's appearance. Would he be leaning on the cane that Matt had drawn? How about his teeth? Would he be all gums like in the cartoon?

"I hope he has creepy spots on him like my grandfather," added Craz. "Did you give him any of those?"

Matt looked at the drawing. "Not yet." He took out the pen and quickly added a few ugly blemishes to his cartoon of the crooked old guy. "That should do it!"

"Hank," screeched Mr. Nuss from behind the kitchen doors. "Look at you. This is terrible!"

The swinging door opened, and a visibly upset Mr. Nuss rushed out into the diner. "I just can't believe this," he said.

A second later the kitchen door opened again. Both Matt and Craz leaned forward, excited to see the results of the pen's magic. From their booth they watched as a hunched-over form slowly backed his way out of the kitchen. He seemed ancient from the way he hobbled slowly backward into the diner.

"Finally my brother's gonna *look* the way he acts!" Craz said, clearly excited.

"All because of this," Matt said, the pen clutched tightly in his fist.

Unfortunately, their excitement instantly fizzled when the bent-over figure straightened up and turned around. There stood an upset but otherwise normal-looking Hank, his apron covered in a mess of dirty dish slop from the splattering of the broken dishes.

"I'm sorry, Mr. Nuss," Hank muttered. "I must've slipped on some french fry grease. I'll pay for the broken dishes. I insist you take it out of my paycheck."

"No," Craz said, slamming his hand onto the table. "The dork is supposed to be old."

"I don't get it," said Matt as he inspected the pen as if he'd see some flaw there. "It worked with the locker and the money. Why not Hank?"

They watched as Hank grabbed a mop from behind the diner counter and dutifully disappeared back into the kitchen.

So much for magic.

THE BOYS PAID THE BILL AND LEFT A BIG TIP. Why not? Maybe they hadn't figured out exactly how Matt's cartoon had turned into a real stash of cash, but feeling like big spenders cheered them up.

When they stepped outside, the afternoon sun felt warm on their backs. And with a backpack full of money, Craz and Matt couldn't be happier.

"Five bucks says I can hit the stop sign with a rock." Craz picked up a small stone and bounced it in his hand. "Did I say five? Let's make it ten."

"Craz, you're a terrible shot," said Matt. "But I can't

resist the bet, even if you'll be paying me with our money."

Craz narrowed his gaze and used his thumb to line up the stop sign on the corner. "Piece of cake," he said as he pulled his arm back and whipped the rock with everything he had.

They waited for the sound of the rock hitting the metal sign, but it never came.

"Pay up," Matt said as he grabbed at the backpack. "On second thought, keep your money. Then spend it on me!"

Craz almost cracked a smile, but he stopped as he looked past Matt's shoulder, where a bunch of bees were starting to form an angry swarm. "Guess my aim really is lousy. I think I hit a beehive."

Matt froze. "Beehive?"

"Yeah. Don't worry. They'll probably go away."

Matt heard the buzzing now, and it was getting louder. "Craz, aren't you forgetting something?" Matt didn't even dare blink, and his fists were clenched in tight balls. "Bees? Plus me . . . equals dead kid."

Now it was Craz's turn to freeze up. "Right. The allergy thing. Totally brain-burped it. Sorry."

Matt slowly reached into his shirt and pulled out a

white penlike thing that was attached to a string hanging around his neck. "You know what to do if I get stung, right? You didn't forget about *that*?"

Craz knew about the EpiPen, which held a shot of medicine that would counteract the effects of an allergic bee sting. Matt had nearly died once when they were six. Craz still remembered the way Matt's face had swelled up and how he'd suddenly had a hard time breathing. It was really scary. After that Matt's mom had made Matt promise to always carry the EpiPen with him, and she'd drilled Craz so that he'd know how to use it too.

Just in case.

Sudden movements would draw the bees' attention, so Matt turned his head in slow motion. He saw them, all right. About two dozen bees swarming a pile of garbage, which thankfully had grabbed their attention.

Craz knew what to do. "Run?"

Matt nodded. "Run!"

16

SHOPPING SPREE

"PROBABLY SHOULDN'T HAVE EATEN SO MANY fries," Craz wheezed once they'd rounded the corner and felt safe from the bees. "Or milk shakes."

"I hate being so allergic," Matt said between gasps of air. "Totally bites."

"You mean *stings*," Craz said with a smile.

Matt didn't laugh. "Craz, how can you forget I'm deathly allergic to bees? I still remember the first time you cut your elbow at day care. Mrs. Stillman gave you a Bugs Bunny Band-Aid."

"That was a great Band-Aid," Craz said, not even aware that he was rubbing his elbow. "Look, I'm sorry I forgot about the bee thing. My brain is just so full that sometimes the important stuff gets pushed into the back."

Matt shook his head. "Whatever." He tucked the EpiPen back inside his shirt.

"Come on. Let me make it up to you," Craz said. "I know the perfect antidote to being chased by bees."

Craz led the way to Sweet-Treats for a twenty-dollar party of candy including, but not limited to, sour cherry bubble-gum balls, red licorice twists, chocolate-covered nut clusters, two pounds of jelly beans, and a bag of gummi bears big enough to make a crater-size cavity!

Craz paid with a random handful of bills grabbed from inside his backpack. The woman behind the counter eyed the boys at first, but Matt told her the money was from their paper route, which seemed to ease any suspicions she had over why two kids had so many loose dollar bills.

Next stop was Denholms, a small store on Highland Avenue that sold men's and boys' clothes.

"Underwear?" Matt asked, staring at his friend. "We can get *anything*, and that's what you buy?"

Craz was standing in line to pay. "My mother refuses to buy me boxers, and I really think it's time to say sayonara to my Spider-Man briefs."

"No argument from me," Matt said. "No wonder you always change in your gym locker."

"Bingo," said Craz, happily clutching two packages of plaid boxer shorts. "Remember this day, Matt. Today I am a man."

Between the candy, underwear, and food feast at the Shack, they had made a decent dent in the cash bag, and so both decided to use what was left to buy Matt something he'd always wanted—a real drawing table.

Easel & Brush was the town's only art supply store. Located at the end of downtown, the brightly lit shop stocked everything from clumps of modeling clay to blank white canvases. High shelves lined three aisles crammed full of painting supplies, pens and pencils, inks, gum erasers, and different-size drawing pads.

Matt loved the smell of Easel & Brush. There was always a faint odor of artist paint in the air mixed with the scent of fresh sheets of paper. When he was little, his dad used to bring him to the store on his Saturday morning errands. Matt remembered getting lost looking at the exotic supplies, most of which he'd never seen before. He'd spent hours inspecting the soft tips of the various brushes and walking among the watercolor sets, rows of colored pencils, and tubes of different kinds and colors of paint. Just being in the store always brought back a happy feeling of a time when his family was whole and when a gift of a little plastic pencil sharpener would make him smile for weeks.

The back of the store opened into a wide space filled with the larger objects that didn't fit on shelves. Here were the fancy swivel chairs that raised and lowered at the touch of a lever, large artist easels that stood taller than a kid, empty frames just waiting to be filled with finished art, and of course, an assortment of drawing tables. For years Matt had longingly walked around the tables, imagining what it would be like to sit behind one like a real cartoonist, but he'd always known that the steep prices were way out of his league.

Today was different.

"Forty-eight dollars," said Craz. "That's all the cash we've got left."

Matt eyed the drawing table price tags. "That easily rules out the Prestige-Elite." Matt stood by the nicest table in the store. "This puppy goes for three hundred forty dollars." Still hopeful, Matt walked among the half dozen other tables. "These others are pretty pricey too."

"Sorry, dude. I really wanted to see you behind one of these bad boys." Craz was spinning around on an expensive chair that cost as much as two drawing tables combined. He gnawed on a twist of red licorice. "Hey, what about that one?" Craz was pointing into a dark corner of the room.

Though most of the tables boasted extra features like spacious drawers and extra shelves for inks and paper, Matt now saw the simple white table with the adjustable legs so you could make the drawing surface slant at whatever angle was most comfortable. This table was a bit smaller than the other ones and was covered in a layer of dust, suggesting it might be an older, less popular model. Matt lifted the price tag, and his face lit up.

"Fifty-two bucks," he read. "That's a heck of a lot closer to what we've got."

"Yeah, but we're still four bills shy. You think they'll take a bag of jelly beans as a trade-in?"

"Worth a shot," Matt said as he dragged the table into the center of the room and then carried it to the cash register in the front of the store.

Delores Tuttle was the cashier and also the manager. She looked over the drawing table while thoughtfully chewing on the inside of her cheek. "Tell you what, seeing how it's one of last year's tables, I'll let it go for forty-five dollars. What do you say?"

Matt was about to seal the deal, but Craz spoke up fast. "We'll give you forty. Even."

Delores didn't bat an eye. "Fine. Forty it is. Free delivery, too."

"Great," said Matt. "I wasn't sure how I was going to get it home."

Delores looked at her watch. "Well, my driver is about to make the last deliveries of the day. If you boys want, you can ride along and get dropped off with the table."

"Sweet," said Craz. "Here, have a gum ball."

THE BOYS STOOD IN THE EASEL & BRUSH PARKING
lot waiting for the delivery van to come around from
behind the store.

It was only four thirty, and the setting sun was a
reminder that the days were getting shorter and that
winter wasn't too far away. The leaves still clung to
a few trees here and there. Fall would be over soon
enough.

"The good news is, I finally have a real drawing
table," Matt said, his mouth full of gummi bears.

"Right," said Craz. "And I guess the bad news is, we
still have no idea how the cartoon you drew became
real."

"I'd like to believe it had something to do with the
cartooning kit," said Matt. "But come on, Craz. A magic
pen?"

Craz stopped tearing a bright yellow maple leaf into
tiny shreds. "Okay, so it obviously isn't some simple thing
with the pen," Craz said. "But you did make it happen,
Matt. It had to be you."

The Easel & Brush delivery van pulled around the building and stopped in front of the boys.

"It would be cool if the magic was because of me," Matt said as he opened the passenger-side door. "But you saw what happened with Hank. Nothing."

The boys climbed in next to the heavyset driver who was squeezed behind the wheel. He turned to the boys, flashed a toothy grin, and said, "You know what I say? Sometimes nothing *is* something."

The boys looked closer at the delivery driver.

It was Boyd T. Boone.

17

OLD MAN HANK

"BOYD T. BOONE! IT WAS YOU!" CRAZ SAID,
bouncing up and down on the front seat of the delivery
van.

"You betcha!" The cartoonist smiled at the boys.
"Everyone buckled?" He glanced at the side mirror, then
zoomed haphazardly into the traffic.

A stunned Matt turned to Craz. "Wait a second.
You've seen him before?"

"Yeah, earlier today. At school," Craz admitted. "But I
was positive it was all just a sugar-fueled mirage. I mean,
I *do* have an overactive imagination. And come on. He
was wearing a dress."

"Actually it was a smock," Boyd T. Boone said. "Big difference. Hey, who wants a hairnet?"

He pulled a mesh lunch-lady hairnet out of his coat pocket and handed it to Matt, who was still trying to get his head around having the strange cartoonist as their driver.

Boyd T. Boone spun the wheel to the left, and the van squealed onto Midland Street, barely avoiding a head-on collision with a Volkswagen. "Nothing like the open road to clear one's sinuses," he said as he turned on the radio. "So, what'll it be? Classic rock or oldies?"

Matt snapped the radio off. "How about we skip the music and you tell us what's going on!"

Boyd T. Boone consulted his clipboard. "Well, what's going on is, first we stop at Three-Five-Six Magnolia Avenue, where we drop off a filing cabinet for a Mr. Peter H. Figgins, and then, if I'm not mistaken, it's just a short two blocks to your house, where *someone* finally has himself a brand-new drawing table." He winked at Matt.

"That's not what I mean," Matt snapped, getting more upset. "The pen. The bag of money.... You!"

"Yes, it can be a little overwhelming. But you'll get

used to it." Boyd T. Boone nodded, then leaned toward the boys. "Mine really is the best cartooning kit available. One of a kind, wouldn't you say?"

Craz reached into his backpack and pulled out the two cartoons Matt had drawn. "Totally!" Craz held up the "Cartoon Kings" comic. "Pretty sweet. I mean, Matt drew it, and then BAM! A bag full of money . . . for free!"

"That is pretty sweet," Boyd T. Boone agreed as he swerved in and out of the traffic.

Matt jumped in. "Okay. Let's just say the pen is magic." He suddenly felt silly for even saying that out loud. Magic? He didn't believe in that stuff. "How come it only worked once? With the money in my locker?"

Boyd T. Boone signaled right but turned left. For a great cartoonist, he was a terrible driver. "If I simply told you the answer, it would take away all the fun of figuring it out." He leaned toward the boys. "But I will say, the pen does have its special qualities. And don't forget the ink. That stuff is pretty potent!"

"Stop sign!" Craz yelled, pointing out the front window at the fast-approaching busy intersection.

Boyd slammed on the brakes, making the van skid to

a stop. "Well, that was fun," he said, his cheeks flushed and his eyes wide open.

Craz held up the place mat. "We also drew my stupid brother as an old man. But it didn't work. He didn't turn old."

Boyd eased the van back into traffic. "Of course he didn't."

Matt was confused. "But I used the same pen. The same ink ..."

Boyd T. Boone lifted one eyebrow suggestively. "Maybe something happened with one cartoon that didn't happen with the other."

The boys looked at each other, trying to remember.

"Maybe it's the paper," said Craz. "Matt made the first cartoon on regular paper but the Hank cartoon was drawn on a dirty place mat. Is that it?"

"In my experience," Boyd T. Boone said with a little shrug, "paper is paper."

Matt was thinking. "Okay. I drew the first cartoon at home ... brought it to school ... then what?"

"Then we wanted to show it to Skip," Craz added. "But first—"

"We made a copy. In the teachers' lounge." Matt turned to Craz. "Did anything weird happen there?"

Boyd T. Boone kept his eyes on the road, but a sly smile snuck onto his face.

"Wait a second," said Craz. "There was this bright flash of light from the copy machine. Is that when the cartoon got real?"

"We have a winner!" Boyd T. Boone shouted a little too loudly. "First you use the pen and the ink. But then you have to make a copy!"

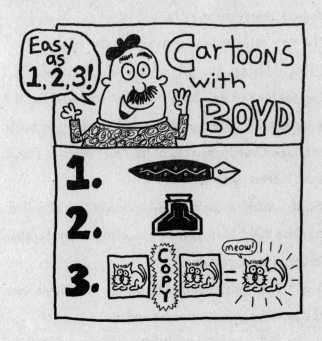

Craz gave himself a thumbs-up for getting the right answer, but Matt was still trying to put the pieces together.

"But what does copying the cartoon have to do with making the magic happen?"

"Just everything," Boyd T. Boone responded. "The only way to spread your comics to other eyeballs is to make copies, right? That's the way this all works. Once your original comic gets duplicated, whatever you draw will actually happen. That's cartooning the Boyd T. Boone way. Pretty great, right?"

The van came to a surprisingly easy stop at a red light that was opposite a bus stop where Hank stood waiting for his bus ride home. He was still wearing the dirty apron and stained pants from the mess he'd made at the Shack. Craz looked out at his older brother. Hank, as usual, looked pathetic.

"So if I made a copy of this cartoon," Craz asked, waving the "Old Man Hank" place mat, "my brother would turn into a grandpa?"

"Yup." The light changed to green, and Boyd shot into the passing lane. "Wrinkles and all."

"Stop the van!" Craz shouted.

Boyd T. Boone obeyed the order and jammed the van into an empty parking space on the side of the street. Excited, Craz threw the door open and jumped out onto the sidewalk.

"What are you doing?" yelled Matt.

"Finishing what we started," Craz said with a grin. "Copy-Copy is a block away. Come on!"

Matt turned to the cartoonist behind the wheel. "Just wait here, okay?"

"Fine and dandy," Boyd T. Boone said. "But mind if I help myself?" He lifted the Sweet-Treats bag of candy and licked his lips. "I'm a sucker for nut clusters."

"Go to town, dude." Matt slammed the door and took off after Craz.

18

BRAINSTORM

THE BOYS ARRIVED OUT OF BREATH AT THE copy shop. Craz clutched the "Old Man Hank" drawing.

"Closing up in five minutes, fellas," Mr. Hupt called from the back of the store, where he was trying to clear a paper jam on one of the big copiers that did huge printing jobs, like restaurant menus and calendars. Easy jobs were handled by the self-serve machine up front.

Matt dug a dime out from his pants pocket. "What if it doesn't work?"

"What if it does?" asked Craz as he placed the drawing facedown onto the copier's glass. He closed the lid and took the dime from Matt. "Here goes nothing."

Craz dropped the dime into the coin slot and then hit the green copy button. First came the familiar sound of the machine warming up, and then the *whoosh* of the scanner traveling beneath the glass, accompanied by the blast of light from under the lid.

"Wait for it," said Craz just before the second, brighter flash filled the room with an audible *Pop.*

Matt couldn't help but gasp. "Was that it?" he asked as the copy of the cartoon fell into the tray.

Craz lifted the copy machine lid and grabbed the original. "Let's go find out!"

They ran outside, hoping to find Hank transformed into a bent-over senior citizen, but rounding the corner, all they saw was the bus pulling away from the stop. Hank was already on the bus.

"Not fair!" Craz cried. "I have to know if it worked!"

Matt grabbed his friend by the shoulder. "I don't think you have to worry. Look."

Sure enough, as the bus passed by, they saw the off-balance figure of an old man wearing the food-stained apron ricocheting from seat to seat like a pinball. Hank was eighty years old. At least.

It was only a glimpse, but enough proof to give both boys a sense that they could do anything.

All they had to do was draw.

"So now what?" asked Matt as the bus disappeared around the corner. "Do we just leave Hank like that?"

"No way," Craz said. "My parents would freak if that geezer walked in the door for dinner. Maybe we should, you know, just doodle him back to normal?"

"No problem!" Matt took the pen from his shirt pocket, then did a quick cartoon in his sketchbook. They ran back into Copy-Copy and spent another dime making sure Hank became young again.

Craz and Matt raced back to the delivery van, excited that the pen had actually worked. The code was cracked. All it took was a copier.

"I wish we could've seen his face when he turned back into a kid," said Craz. "Had to be priceless."

"Unbelievable," Matt said as he twirled the pen in his fingers. "We are so going to rule our school!"

"Forget school," said Craz. "Let's rule the world!"

They ran up to the Easel & Brush van and opened the door to get in.

"Took you long enough," the man behind the wheel said.

Matt's jaw dropped. "But you're not . . ."

"I'm not what?" asked the driver, a grumpy gray-haired fellow who clearly was not Boyd T. Boone. "Let's get this show on the road. My fish aren't going to feed themselves."

Craz pulled on Matt's arm. "Happened before too. Now you see him . . . now you don't. Just go with it."

After first delivering the file cabinet, the driver stopped in front of Matt's house. "Hope you don't think I'm lugging that table inside for you," the cranky driver said. "You're on your own, buckoes."

Matt and Craz didn't really care. They both had one thing on their mind. Cartooning!

"Supper in ten minutes," Matt's mom said as soon as the boys walked in. "Are you eating with us, Larry?"

Before Craz could say "Of course," Matt jumped in. "No time, Mom. Big project due. We already ate, anyway."

"But I love your mom's cooking," Craz said. "She knows how to not burn things."

"Here," Matt said, pushing the bag of candy at Craz. "Now you have supper."

Craz was all smiles.

The first thing they did was set up the drawing table and rearrange the space in Matt's room so that the new table could be in easy reach of Matt's desk, where he had neatly laid out the pen, bottle of ink, and a stack of blank paper.

"Okay," said Craz, pacing back and forth. "What do we draw first?"

"Easy," said Matt. "I make a comic where we become the cartoonists for the *Lantern*."

Matt grabbed a sheet of paper and lifted the pen.

"Yeah, that's one way to go," Craz carefully said as he grabbed the pen from Matt and held it up like it was something Indiana Jones had just found in a cave of ancient ruins. "I'm thinking maybe we should go bigger."

"Bigger?"

"Sure. Let's come up with some really wild stuff first!"

Matt bit his lip. "But the school paper. We could make it happen."

Craz spun Matt in his chair. "Plenty of time for that.

How about we just let our minds wander a little first? Brainstorm on it."

Matt chewed it over. There was no harm in brainstorming. "Anything goes, right?"

"That's the brainstorming rule," said Craz, ready to write down whatever they came up with. *"Anything!"*

Craz took a handful of candy, threw it into his mouth, and then as the sweet flavors mingled, he began to let the ideas flow. "Okay. Let's draw us two new computers! The really pricey kind. With amazingly sick touch screens," he said.

"Flying machines," added Matt, getting into it. "Oh, and how about our own theme park? With no lines to get on the best rides!"

"Yeah. And a mustache!" Craz touched his upper lip and imagined how cool he'd look with one. "Oooh! How about a huge flat-screen TV and new Wii, PlayStation, and Xboxes? And every game ever made. And awesome snacks! No, a soda machine and a McDonald's in my bedroom. Wait, I wouldn't need the soda machine if I had my own Mickey Dees. Scratch the soda and make it an all-you-can-eat bacon buffet!"

"Bacon buffet?" asked Matt.

"We said anything goes. And I do love my bacon!"

They tossed out ideas for an hour. The wilder, the better. And why not? They had a pen that could draw *anything* they wanted. The sky was the limit, so why not shoot for the moon?

"My own rocket ship," Matt said. "That would be twisted!"

"Do you think the pen works in zero gravity?"

"Sure. If I draw that it does, it will."

The door burst open, and Ricky and Foomer filled the frame. "There you are," Ricky said, picking at his teeth. "Mom said you have to do the dishes."

"Yeah, dishes," snickered the ever-annoying Foomer.

"But I didn't even eat supper," said Matt. "No fair."

"Tough luck, chump." Ricky grinned. "I'd say 'Take it up with Mom,' but she went out. Left me in charge. And I say it's time to wash the dishes."

Ricky high-fived Foomer and then slammed the door shut.

"No way your mom said to do the dishes. That's all Ricky."

"Tell me something I don't know," Matt said, and fumed. "He thinks he's the boss of me. I wish I could get back at him."

The idea hit Craz first. He sat up on the bed. "You *can* get back at him, Matt!"

A smile slowly spread on Matt's face. He reached for the pen. "Yeah, I can, can't I?" He unscrewed the cap and then grabbed a new sheet of paper. "Poor Ricky," he said, the perfect idea for revenge already forming in his brain.

19

TAKE THAT!

THE CARTOON LOOKED GREAT. NOW ALL MATT
and Craz had to do was find someplace to get it copied.

"Too bad we can't just make a dupe of it here," said
Matt. "Copy-Copy's closed, and the library is too far of
a walk."

Craz looked around Matt's bedroom. "Hold on," he
said. "Maybe there is a way."

Matt watched Craz get off the bed and then reach
up to the top shelf of his bookcase where Matt kept his
scanner. Craz carried the boxy scanner over to Matt's
desk. "Boyd T. Boone said the magic works when we
duplicate the cartoon. He didn't say it had to be from a
copy machine."

Craz plugged the scanner into the wall socket and then attached it to Matt's computer with the USB cord. "A scan is a copy, right?"

Matt opened the lid and slid the cartoon of Ricky and Foomer onto the glass. "We've got nothing to lose."

They waited for the scanner to warm up and then pushed the button on the side of the machine. A low whirr sound filled the room, followed by the blink of bright light signaling that the image had been digitized. A second flash of light shot out from beneath the lid.

"That's a good sign," said Craz as he watched the duplicate image of the new cartoon load onto Matt's computer screen. "Sure looks like a copy to me."

In the kitchen Ricky was in the middle of a story about how he'd made his history teacher cry, when he suddenly dropped the bag of corn chips he was feeding on and uncontrollably stood up from the table. "You know what I want to do, Foomer?"

Foomer, who was now a baboon in a diaper, answered, "Clean the house, bro!"

"You look weird," said Ricky, unable to stop himself from putting on his mom's girliest apron and filling the sink with soapy water. "And why are you a monkey?"

"Beats me," said Foomer as he swung from the light fixture and landed feetfirst next to the bananas in the bowl on the counter. "But I sure wish I was vacuuming right now."

Matt and Craz snuck out from the bedroom and watched from the hallway while Ricky scrubbed an endless stack of dirty pots and pans and baboon Foomer pushed the vacuum cleaner around the living room while he scratched himself all over.

"I think I could get real used to this kind of cartooning," said Matt.

"I already am," added Craz. "Come on. I think I know exactly what we need to draw next."

They headed back to Matt's bedroom, where Craz laid out his plan.

"As great as it would be to draw portable spaceships and kangaroo jumping boots and mind-reading robots, maybe we should concentrate on something we don't just want but really *need*."

Matt thought hard. "Like getting straight As?"

"Better than that," said Craz. "How about making us the perfect Saturday night!"

Matt tried to picture what Craz wanted. "Craz, I'm not drawing an alien invasion with us as commando jet fighters or something totally nuts like that."

"Fine," Craz said, just slightly disappointed. "But what about a night where you get to hang out with Cindy? Wouldn't that be nice?"

"Yeah," Matt admitted. "That would be awesome. But what about you? Who would you want to hang out with?"

Craz clapped a hand on Matt's shoulder and smiled. "Oh, I'm sure I can think of someone."

20

GETTING READY

SATURDAY NIGHT ROLLED AROUND, AND THE boys had cleaned up—well, at least by their standards. Matt wore a shirt that was actually ironed (thank you very much, Foomer!), and Craz had gone back and forth for an hour about whether or not he should wear a cape.

"Too much?" Craz asked, posing with his hands in the air. "I am so stoked. I want to show off my fan-boy excitement without blasting a spotlight on my inner geek." He leaned over Matt's shoulder. "Is the comic finished?"

"Done!" Matt grabbed the new cartoon. He smiled at the thought that, thanks to the strange, magical cartooning kit, he was finally going to go hang out with Cindy Ockabloom.

"Way to go, Matt," Craz said, looking over the cartoon. "And nice job with Captain G-Force. You really nailed the cyborg helmet."

"It's the least I could do." Matt beamed. "I get to spend a night with Cindy. You get to hang with your favorite superhero. Perfect Saturday night."

"You got that right!" Craz said, pointing at the drawing. "Great idea adding Captain G's Quantum Accel-a-car, by the way."

"Yeah, I thought using his ride would be a pretty classy way to get around town," said Matt. He raised the lid of the scanner and took one last look at the panels of his cartoon. "First a quick dinner where I don't have to make too much conversation."

"I hear you. Not talking to girls is something I'm really good at," Craz said. "No worries, though. I've got a million questions for the captain. I can keep the convo going strong."

"Great. Then after dinner we cruise to the Imperial and spend a couple of hours watching a romantic movie inside a dark theater, hand-holding optional."

"Speak for yourself!" Craz didn't want to hold hands,

but he definitely wanted to try on Captain G-Force's crime-fighting gravity gloves.

Matt looked at the last panel and sighed. "The perfect Saturday night."

"Sounds decent enough. But . . ." Craz rubbed his chin. "Only thing I'd change is the movie. Chick-flicks are so boring. Maybe you should amp it up."

"Amp it up? How?"

Craz grabbed the cartoon and thought for a second. "Simple. Make it a scary movie. Something that gets the heart pumping, you know?"

Matt liked Craz's idea but hated the thought of having to redo the whole cartoon. "It's a ton of work to start over, and it's already five thirty."

As usual, Craz had the solution. "You don't have to redraw the whole thing. Just add something to the last panel. Have Cindy say, 'That was the scariest movie ever.' That'll take care of it, right?"

Matt eyed the cartoon and saw that he could easily squeeze in a speech balloon. "Sure. Why not? Let the movie be scary." He was already picturing how Cindy would snuggle closer to him. "Hand me the pen."

Matt added the simple line of dialogue for Cindy and then slid the cartoon under the scanner lid. "Here's to finally getting a great Saturday night!"

"You and me, buddy," Craz said, thrusting his fist into the air like Captain G-Force. "And a night to remember!"

21

SATURDAY NIGHT

DINNER WENT PRETTY MUCH AS THEY HAD drawn it—a cozy table for four in the corner of Pizelli's Pizza House. Nothing fancy that might make anyone uncomfortable, and plenty of choices for food—as long as they included crust, sauce, and cheese.

Cindy looked pretty in a jean skirt and purple sweater, and Matt didn't even have to draw that part.

"Great pick for dinner," Cindy said with a bite of Hawaiian pizza dripping from her mouth. "I'm really glad you called, Matt."

"And I'm really glad you didn't hang up on me," Matt said, instantly wishing he could try that sentence again, only this time without sounding like a jerk.

"This carbohydrate-based sustenance makes my circuits dance," Captain G-Force announced from across the table, looking chiseled and perfect, except for the napkin tucked in as a bib to keep his neon purple uniform sauce-free. Famished, the cyborg superhero was already working on his second whole veggie party pizza. "Yum. I've never actually eaten food before."

"I know," Craz said with a full mouth. "How come comic books never show you guys eating? What's that about?"

"I've never used a bathroom before either. But that's all about to change for . . . Captain G-Force!" He stood up and carefully wiped the sauce from his mouth. "This truly is an exciting day."

As the superhero made his way to the men's room, Cindy leaned in to Matt. "Craz's uncle is kind of strange, isn't he?"

"I think it runs in the family," Matt said as he watched Craz try on Captain G-Force's

gravity gloves and then punch at invisible enemies. "But what are friends for, right?"

Cindy smiled. "Right."

After dessert they piled into the sleek Accel-a-car, and Captain G-Force used the quantum drive to zoom them to the Imperial theater across town. The Imperial was one of those old-time movie houses with just one screen, and they popped their popcorn fresh instead of pouring it out of huge plastic bags like at the megaplex in the mall.

"Facemelters 3-D?" Cindy read the title from the theater's marquee while Craz bought tickets. "Sounds kind of scary."

"Not to worry, young lady," Captain G-Force said with his hands squarely on his hips. "Scary is my middle name!"

Matt pulled Cindy aside. "Scary is good, right?" Matt looked a little worried.

Cindy grinned. "Are you kidding? Scary is great!" She gave his arm a little squeeze. "I love being scared."

Craz gave Matt a *Told ya* nod and then pushed Captain G-Force through the open glass doors. "It's showtime!"

At the snack bar they loaded up on two tubs of popcorn with real butter, a box of Raisinets, and four huge sodas. "Our treat," Craz announced. It was a good thing Matt had drawn them a fresh supply of cash.

They went to find seats in the theater but stopped when a malted milk ball bonked Matt in the head. He turned around and saw Paulie Frick grinning from an aisle seat next to some of his Killer Bees football buddies.

"You boys sure you can handle a movie like this?" Paulie shouted so that lots of people were staring at Matt and Craz. "It's not a cartoon, you know. And what's with the big weirdo in the cheapo costume? Halloween was last month, dude."

Craz exploded. "Cheapo costume? He's wearing an original one-of-a-kind Captain G-Force cyber suit. They don't come any more real than this!"

Paulie tossed another malted milk ball, which hit Captain G-Force in the chest. "Bull's-eye!"

"You, sir, shall be annihilated!" Captain G-Force touched his left gravity glove, which began to vibrate and glow a deep crimson.

"Uh, no. That's okay, Captain," Craz quickly said. "Let's just get some seats."

The glove went back to normal. "As you wish, short companion."

"Bye-bye, babies," Paulie shouted before laughing loudly. "Losers."

Matt tensed up. His shoulders pushed closer to his ears.

"Just ignore him," Cindy said. "He's been a jerk since fourth grade. He's not worth it." Her voice was so sweet that Matt relaxed a little as they continued looking for a place to sit.

They settled into four seats near the screen just as the lights went down and the trailers began. Captain G-Force was going wild on the popcorn and enjoyed how the soda made him burp.

After about ten minutes of mostly boring movie previews, *Facemelters* finally started and everyone in the theater put on the 3-D glasses. Electronic music echoed softly and then swooped to a loud clash of instruments as the title of the movie shot off the screen and then melted, which looked like it was dripping onto their laps.

"Gross." Cindy laughed. She reached into the popcorn at the same moment Matt did, and their hands touched. She didn't pull away, and Matt didn't dare even move a finger.

This was going to be a great night.

The first twenty minutes of the movie were pretty lame. A scientist named Dr. Lutzor was in a horrible accident and had burns all over his body. His face was totally disfigured, and he became a recluse in his lab. Working to create a fake skin to fix his own face, he accidentally created living flesh that mutated and started to consume any human it came in contact with. There was a subplot with zombies, which actually made no sense.

"And the really scary stuff hasn't even started yet," Craz whispered to Matt.

Surprisingly, Boyd T. Boone had a cameo as a pizza delivery guy who gets eaten by the zombies, and then Dr. Lutzor barricaded himself in his lab as he cooked up a new vat of skin.

"Fresh flesh!" he screamed, holding up a handful of the drippy ooze, which he shoved out into the audience.

"Ewww," groaned the entire theater, except Captain G-Force, who shouted, "Annihilate!"

Dr. Lutzor then picked up a scary-looking needle filled with some sort of fluorescent sci-fi formula and injected the skin, making it wriggle and pulse in his hand before he slapped the liquid mess onto his charred face and screamed in pain as the growing skin began to meld onto his skull with a disgusting wet sucking sound.

Cindy was folded up against Matt. She had her hand over her 3-D glasses. "Can I look? Is that icky stuff still oozing?"

"Oh, yeah," said Matt, staring at the screen, where the doctor was now leaning out into the audience with his new flesh-face melting.

Craz elbowed Matt. "I gotta admit, this is the best 3-D I've ever seen. It's so real."

"I know," Matt said. "I swear I can feel his face actually dripping on my head."

That was the moment that Cindy chose to open her eyes again. She screamed at the image of Dr. Lutzor's creepy melting face.

And then she screamed again when she took off the

3-D glasses and realized his face really was melting off the screen and onto the audience.

"Ahhhh!" Cindy screamed along with the rest of the theater audience.

"Setting gravity glove to laser!" shouted Captain G-Force, who stood up on his chair, prepared for battle.

"This is so cool," Craz said while he snapped pictures of the craziness with his cell phone.

Matt whipped off his 3-D glasses and watched the entire audience start to panic as Dr. Lutzor made slicing motions at them with his scalpel. Adding to the insanity, Captain G-Force began shooting his glove laser wildly at the screen. People were running for the exits, and Paulie Frick was actually hiding under his seat, which was the only thing in the chaos that made Matt smile.

"Take me home," Cindy insisted as soon as they had found their way into the theater lobby. She grabbed a handful of napkins and wiped some of the slimy, oozy stuff off her nice sweater. "I can't believe you took me here!"

Because Captain G-Force and Craz stayed behind to fight Dr. Lutzor and the zombies, Matt and Cindy were forced to take a bus back to her house. It was a long, uncomfortable ride, and neither of them could find anything to say.

"I thought you liked scary movies," Matt finally said once they were standing on Cindy's front porch.

"Everyone likes being scared *a little*," Cindy said, still upset and acting cold to Matt. "That was the scariest movie ever!"

Matt remembered those were the exact words that he'd put into the cartoon. Except in the cartoon Cindy was smiling, and right now she could barely look at him.

"I wish I'd stayed home," she said before storming into her house, leaving Matt alone on the porch, which wasn't exactly the way he'd pictured that the evening would end.

22

BACK TO NORMAL?

AS SOON AS HE GOT HOME, MATT USED THE pen to draw a new cartoon that erased the Saturday night disaster and then did a quick scan of it to make sure it became real right away.

Thankfully, Cindy would now have no memory of the 3-D movie meltdown and Matt could go back to the safety of worshiping her silently from afar.

"It's our fault," Matt said from the kitchen phone the next morning. "We made it the scariest movie ever. Who knew the pen would turn it into a total horror show."

"I miss Captain G-Force," Craz whined. "He was going to show me his secret lair."

"I'm sorry," Matt said. "But I had to redraw it so the whole evening went away. But I'll get you a new Captain G-Force action figure to make up for it, okay?"

"The expensive one with the working laser gravity glove?"

"Sure. I'll doodle it later."

"Fine," Craz sighed. "So now what? Are you going to try again with Cindy? Maybe doodle up a little miniature golfing? A picnic is always safe, though kind of dorky."

"No way," Matt said. "I'm not using the pen to get her to like me. If it happens, it happens."

"If you say so," Craz said. After an awkward moment of silence he got excited. "So what should we draw up today? Jet packs? A caveman butler?"

"Hello? Are you even listening? We just barely survived last night. No more crazy cartoons," Matt said. "Besides, it's Sunday. I have to hang with my family."

"Riiiiight," Craz said. "I forgot you guys have that whole 'family day' thing at your house. Even with your dad gone, you guys still do it, huh?"

Matt snuck a look at his mother sitting alone on the living room couch doing her Sunday crossword puzzle.

"Yup. Another Sunday fun day," Matt said. "What are you up to?"

"Me?" Craz watched as his little sister kicked his little brother, who then ripped off her doll's head and bit into it like a bagel. Meagan's scream pierced Craz's brain. "Just looking for a new family."

MATT POKED HIS HEAD INTO RICKY'S ROOM.

"What do you want?" Ricky was lying on his bed reading the new issue of *GuitarMax*. "Come on, spit it out."

"It's just . . . you know. I was wondering . . ."

Ricky stared at Matt. "What? Come on, Matt. You're sucking up my free time."

"Do you ever miss Dad?" Matt finally asked from the safety of the doorway. He knew actually stepping *into* Ricky's room would not end well.

"Does a vampire miss the sunlight?" Ricky snapped. "What's eating you?"

Matt shook his head. "I dunno. Mom seems lonely."

"Mom is fine," said Ricky, who finally looked up from his magazine. "Maybe you're the one with the problem. Ever think of that?"

"Hey, I couldn't care less. I just thought . . ." Matt let his words trail off. What did he think? That his life would be better if his dad had never left? Sure. Why wouldn't that be true? They were happier when they were a whole family; at least he thought so. "Forget it. But we should plan something good for today so Mom doesn't take us to a flower show again."

"Ugh, family day." Ricky let out a deep groan. "I hate Sundays. Now get out of here and close the door. Tight!"

Back in his room Matt picked up the framed family photo from when he was eight. It had been taken at Disneyland, and all four of them stood in front of

Sleeping Beauty's castle against a bright blue sky. He remembered the day as perfect, and the family had never looked happier. Matt couldn't help but think how different everything was back then. Ricky was his best friend. His mom and dad had their arms around each other. He still thought wearing a mouse ears cap with his name sewn on it was cool.

His door opened and his mother stuck her head inside. "What do you say to a trip to the outlet mall? And burgers?"

"Sounds like a plan," Matt replied a little too happily. At least the burger part was something he could handle.

"Great. Twenty minutes. Okay?"

"Can't wait," he lied, knowing nothing could be worse than being dragged to an endless string of outlet stores.

Twenty minutes. That was enough time to read the assigned chapter of *Treasure Island* that was due on Monday. It sure would be good to get that homework off his back. But it was also enough time to make a new cartoon, and Matt had an idea that he thought would be perfect.

He grabbed his new pen and a fresh sheet of paper, and then, staring at the Disneyland photo, he drew a cartoon of himself, his mother, then Ricky, and finally his dad.

One big happy family spending another Sunday together.

23

BRAND-NEW DAY

CRAZ LOCKED HIS BIKE TO THE RACK IN FRONT of Kilgore Junior High. His dad needed to take the family car in to be fixed, so Craz had been forced to get himself to school.

It was rare that he showed up to school on time and even more of a miracle to actually be early. Especially on a Monday, when the morning scene in his house was like one of those slapstick comedies where everyone runs into one another and grabs the wrong lunches while crazed parents scream in the background. But there he was. Ten minutes early and with the right lunch bag in his backpack.

"I'm telling you, Sammy," Craz said, leaning against

the flagpole in front of the school, "I'm lucky to make it here alive. You've seen my bike. That thing is a piece of junk."

Craz pointed to his bike, which had more rust showing than paint.

"Yeah, it has seen better days," Sammy said as he picked a scab off his elbow and then flicked it off his thumb into the grass. "So anything good happen this weekend?"

Craz immediately thought of the wild night he'd had with Captain G-Force but knew there was no point in bragging about it. In the end it never really happened anyway. Even the pictures on his cell phone were gone. Matt's cartoon had made sure of that.

"Nope," Craz said. "The usual weekend stuff. Eat. Sleep. Bathroom. Repeat."

Sammy nodded. "I got grounded for downloading a virus onto my dad's computer, so you know things were wild at my house. Oh, yeah. Good times."

A bright red BMW sports car pulled up to the curb, and much to Sammy's and Craz's surprise, Matt stepped out of the passenger door.

"Since when did Matt start getting rides to school?" asked Sammy. "And since when is his mom a dude?"

Craz was just as surprised to see Matt get out of the car, and he was even more surprised to see that the dude behind the wheel was Matt's dad. He'd moved out of the house months ago, and even though he still lived in town, he'd practically disappeared from Matt's life. And he definitely never drove such a fancy car.

Matt gave his dad a fist bump and then closed the door and waved as the two-seater sports car sped away from the school.

"Hey, guys," Matt said to Sammy and Craz as he walked over to the flagpole.

"That car," said Sammy. "Fancy-shmancy."

Craz squinted at his friend. "Things look pretty chummy with your dad. What's up with that?"

Matt hesitated. "He, uh, moved back home. In fact it's almost like he never left."

"Must've gotten a big raise, too," Craz said somewhat suspiciously. "That was some car."

Matt just shrugged as the first bell rang and the groups of kids hanging out in front of the school started to move, sluglike, through the front doors.

FOR CRAZ THE SCHOOL DAY BEGAN WITH A MAJOR brain fail in his French class, where the verbs seemed to gang up on him. He managed to ask to go to the bathroom in a future-perfect tense that made the other kids in class laugh—so that was a plus, even though he didn't get to use the toilet until after the period ended.

The morning dragged on, and both boys suffered through a health class where the lesson plan centered on the perils of pimples.

As the PowerPoint images of different zits flashed on the smart board, Craz finally brought up what had been on his mind all morning. "Listen, about your dad . . ."

"I know." Matt bit his thumbnail and wouldn't make eye contact with his best friend. "Showing up and patching things up at home. Crazy, right?"

Craz didn't buy it. "You used the pen, didn't you? You drew your father. And that car. Man, that was a nice ride."

Matt looked at Craz. "I had to. It's just . . ." He paused. "It was so easy to do. Just like that, there we were. A whole family again. And yeah, the car. He always wanted one like that, so I figured why not sweeten the deal? Make him happy so that we all can be happy."

"Hey, no harm, no foul from me. I think it's kind of awesome he's back," Craz said.

Matt smiled. "You know, we had the best time yesterday. All four of us. Batting cages. Barbecue ribs. A movie. Even Ricky kind of smiled. We're planning a winter vacation. The Bahamas. My mom's been dying to go there forever, and now . . . it's looking real."

Matt took the pen out of his shirt pocket and tapped it against his open palm. "Who knew fixing a family could be so easy?"

24

TROUBLE

"I STILL DON'T UNDERSTAND WHY THEY DIDN'T just nuke the Hispaniola." Barry Higgins was once again complaining that the *Treasure Island* pirates would make terrible Navy SEALS and that Jim Hawkins, Captain Smollett, and Dr. Livesey were total wusses.

"For the last time, Barry, Robert Louis Stevenson has crafted a work that reflects the times in which he lived," Mrs. Bentz said through clenched teeth. "There were no nuclear weapons. And I think you'll ultimately find the actions of Jim Hawkins rather heroic."

"Fat chance," Barry Higgins said under his breath.

The bell rang and kids immediately gathered books and backpacks. Mrs. Bentz held up her hand, which froze all activity. "Chapters twenty-seven and twenty-eight for tomorrow," she said. "And Mr. Crazinski and Mr. Worfle, please see me after class."

Diesel McKenzie snickered from his seat behind Matt. "Whatever it is, I hope it's trouble."

"Yeah, *big* trouble," echoed Skip Turkle.

Mrs. Bentz turned her back to the class and quickly wrote out the homework on the blackboard. Craz poked Matt on the shoulder.

"What'd we do?" he asked.

"Beats me. But whenever she calls you by your last name, it's never good."

Matt and Craz stayed in their seats as the rest of the kids practically ran for freedom. Diesel stood in the doorway and used his finger to make a slow cut across his throat. He laughed as he joined Skip in the hallway, leaving Matt and Craz alone with the dreaded Mrs. Bentz.

The first thing she did was close the door. Not a good sign.

"Rules exist for good reason," she sternly began. "Would you agree, Lawrence?"

Craz knew they were doomed but thought he'd better play along. "Yes, Mrs. Bentz. I totally agree."

"Good," she said, and then turned her attention on Matt. "And *why* do rules exist, Matthew?"

Matt felt some sweat drip down from his armpit. He hadn't thought he was nervous, but all of a sudden he was sure that he was. "Um . . . Well, for one thing, rules keep order separated from chaos." He didn't know if she'd accept his answer, and suddenly felt like he was on a game show. A game show he was going to lose.

Mrs. Bentz made the "tut-tut" noise that pinched her puckered face even more, signaling that she was not pleased with the answer. Both boys watched as she walked behind her desk and opened her file drawer. She reached inside and pulled out a piece of paper, then showed it to them. It was the "Cartoon Kings" original drawing. The one Craz just then realized he'd forgotten under the copier lid in the teachers' lounge.

"I'm glad you take so much pride in your shenanigans

that you sign your own work." She tapped at their signatures with her sharp fingernail and paused long enough for Matt to feel more sweat dripping inside his shirt. He really needed a better deodorant.

"I found your handiwork in the teachers' lounge copy machine on Friday. How many rules do you think you broke?"

Craz jumped at the answer. "Well, we're not supposed to go into the teachers' lounge, so that's obviously one rule. And we kind of used the copy machine, so that's two." He should've quit talking right there but kept going. "But if you multiply that by Matt and me, I guess the correct answer's gotta be . . . four."

Mrs. Bentz sneered at Craz. "Do you think this is funny, Mr. Crazinski?"

Craz knew what to say, but the logical part of his brain was put into a choke hold by the wise-mouth part. "No, ma'am. What I think is funny is how you read us *Treasure Island* every day and don't even try to add any sound effects or do different voices."

Matt froze in his seat.

Craz put on a cockney accent. "Aye, I'm Jack 'awkins and I'm stuck on a bloomin', bleedin' borin' boat with scallywags and 'oodlums, I am."

Matt was breathing hard and kept his hands folded tight on the desktop. It was one of those moments when he wished his best friend wasn't so weird, but that ship had sailed a long time ago.

Mrs. Bentz stood totally still. Her eyes became tiny and the red-raged anger rose from her neckline all the way up to her forehead. If Matt drew the cartoon of her, there'd be steam coming out from her ears.

"That's it," she said, slamming her file drawer shut. "Detention would just give you two the time to draw more of your insipid cartoons." She waved the "Cartoon Kings" comic like it was dirty laundry. "Rules, gentlemen, need to be followed. One, you snuck into an off-limits school area, and two, you used school machinery without permission. What do you think should be done?"

Matt knew to say nothing, and he also knew Craz was incapable of silence.

"If you ask me," Craz blurted out with one eye

squinted shut like an eye-patched pirate, "make us walk the plank. Eh, matey?" And then he made believe he was a parrot and squawked, "Walk the plank! Walk the plank!"

Matt put his head in his hands while Mrs. Bentz seethed from behind her huge desk. She opened her file drawer and slid the drawing back into a hidden folder.

"Wonderful performance, Lawrence," she said as a tight smile spread on her lips. "I think I know a proper punishment that should suit you both just fine."

25

THE PUNISHMENT

"LOOK, I'M SORRY, OKAY? HOW MANY TIMES DO I have to say it?"

It was between periods and the guys were hanging out in the second-floor boys' bathroom, which was the one where the stalls actually locked. Washing his hands at the bathroom sink, Matt was so mad he couldn't even look at Craz. "How about you just stop talking for once? How does that sound?"

Craz caught Matt's eye in the mirror and opened his mouth to respond, but then quickly shut it. He made a *Zip my lip* move with his fingers and smiled meekly.

"A twenty-page research paper? Tough break," said Sammy, who combed his hair again, trying unsuccessfully to look anything but geeky.

"Twenty pages. Each!" Matt stared at his friends. "And we have to analyze the main characters' motivation for wanting the buried treasure. What does that even mean?"

"Stiff sentencing, if you ask me," added Len, who was leaning against the wall that had once again just been painted to hide the scribbles and graffiti kids always added there. "Bentz is just evil."

Craz listened to the conversation with his lips pursed tightly. He was fighting the urge to jump into the conversation, but the frequent glares from Matt kept him mute.

Sammy nodded. "That's a whopper of an assignment. When's it due?"

"Friday," Matt moaned. "*This* Friday!"

Len and Sammy shared a look. Craz silently shrugged. They all knew that it would be a ton of research on top of all that writing. No fun at all.

"You need a couple of extra days *at least* to tackle this puppy," Len said. "Too bad she won't call in sick. Mrs. Bentz hasn't missed a day of school in three years."

"That's true," added Sammy. "Rumor is that last year she came to work with a hundred-and-four fever. Taught class in a plastic bubble."

Matt shook his head. "We're doomed."

"Hold on," said Len. "Just because she never gets sick doesn't mean she couldn't have a little 'accident.'"

"An *accident*?" Matt stared at his friend. "I'm not putting a hit out on Mrs. Bentz. I just want enough time to get this lame assignment off my back."

Craz had stayed silent long enough. "Maybe she could just go on a sudden vacation," he blurted out. "You know, like to *an island*." Craz looked directly at Matt. He had an idea that would solve all their problems.

"An island?" Matt looked worried.

Craz grinned. "Yeah. Maybe she should go visit Treasure Island."

Sammy and Len laughed. "Treasure Island! Bentz would love that, wouldn't she?"

"Just her and the pirates," Craz said with a wink that only Matt caught.

"Well, I'll tell you one thing. That would definitely get you a substitute teacher," joked Len. "Definitely."

THE GYM WAS DECORATED WITH YELLOW AND
black streamers, and a ton of colorful helium balloons
had been arranged to create an archway over the boys'
locker room door. It was a schoolwide pep rally, and the
bleachers were packed with kids ready to cheer on their
team. The last-period class had been canceled so that
the Killer Bees football players could know just how
much Kilgore Junior High wanted them to beat down
the Brimley Tigers in that afternoon's big football game.

"Who's got the stuff?" shouted the cheerleader squad from the center of the gym.

"Killer Bees!" shouted most of the kids and all of the teachers. "Killer Bees!" they shouted again when the cheerleaders put their hands to their ears in a cheesy *I can't hear you* move.

"Killer Bees!" shouted Coach Arakanian, who felt total devotion to each and every member of his squad . . . as long as they won. When they didn't, he screamed at them until he lost his voice.

The cheerleaders broke off into a pattern of tumbles and flips as Principal Droon walked onto the court. He wore an oversize Killer Bees jersey on top of his suit coat, which made him look ridiculous.

Principal Droon took the microphone off the stand and put it up to his lips. "Bzzzzzzz!" He made the familiar sound of swarming bees.

"Bzzzzzzzz!" responded most of the kids and all of the teachers, so that the gym filled with the imagined threat of a few hundred bee stings, which made Matt touch his EpiPen nervously.

Since the beginning of the rally, Craz had waited in his seat alone at the top of the bleachers, but finally he pushed his way down four rows and past a bunch of kids, who all gave him dirty looks. He stepped on several kids' toes before squeezing in next to Matt. "So, Matt-man. What do you think?"

Matt was still mad at Craz. He answered coolly. "What do I think about *what*?"

"Treasure Island. Mrs. Bentz. It would make an awesome cartoon."

"You were serious?"

"One hundred percent," Craz said. "You said it yourself. We just need a little more time to write the assignment. Besides, think of it from her perspective. How much would she love going there? We'd be giving her a dream come true."

Matt remained skeptical. "You sure that wouldn't be a nightmare?"

Craz looked down at Principal Droon now high-fiving the football players as they ran out from the locker room to the center of the gym.

Craz turned back to Matt. "Look, I know I don't always think things through and that my mouth gets me in trouble sometimes."

Matt fumed. "It isn't just *you*, Craz."

"Right. My mouth gets *us* into trouble. But we've got our hands on something amazing. Don't you think we should use it to help us out?"

Paulie Frick, the Killer Bees quarterback, took the microphone from Principal Droon. "Thanks, Principal Goon," he said, to the cheers of most of the kids but none of the teachers. "Let's kick some Tiger butt today!"

Matt turned to his friend. He sighed. "Truth is . . . I think you have an awesome idea and there's nothing I'd like more than to send Bentz to that stupid island."

"That's what I'm talking about!" Craz shouted above the cheers of the crowd. "I'm telling you, she's going to go nuts about this."

Matt sighed. "And we'll still write the papers?"

"Of course we will. She goes away for a couple days and we get more time. It's a win-win situation."

The pep rally had hit critical mass. Cheerleaders were

jumping and screaming while the football players butted heads and grunted like animals. Coach Arakanian was actually on his hands and knees making believe he was a Brimley Junior High Tiger that the players should try to tackle.

Matt took the pen from his backpack. "Just a little trip to Treasure Island, and then she comes back."

"Yeah," said Craz. "Comes back with a tan and as many doubloons as she can stuff in her girdle!"

While the gym erupted in shouts of "Killer Bees! Killer Bees!" Matt and Craz slipped down the row and out of the gym. They didn't care about a silly football game.

They had a cartoon to create.

26

A SKETCHY GETAWAY

WITH THE WHOLE SCHOOL CONSUMED BY THE PEP rally in the gym, it was easy to slip into the empty library and spread out at one of the back tables to secretly create a quick comic. Craz paced in a tight circle as he carefully crafted the details that Matt drew to guarantee that Mrs. Bentz would become part of the *Treasure Island* story.

"I hope she knows what she's in for," said Matt, inspecting the last panel, where he'd drawn his terrible teacher discovering she was on her beloved island.

"Dude. She's got the book memorized," said Craz. "If anyone knows what she's in for, it's her!"

Matt signed the cartoon and then handed the special

pen to Craz so he could add his name too. "All we need now is to make a copy."

The guys knew they couldn't risk using a school machine again, so Craz took the cartoon and promised to stop by Copy-Copy on his way home and use the self-serve machine there.

"And then it's an island vacation for her and a Bentz-free week for us!" Craz beamed.

The final bell of the day rang, and Matt quickly loaded up his backpack so he could rush off to catch his bus home. "I want to be there when my dad gets off work," Matt shouted as he ran out of the library. "He promised to shoot hoops."

"Laters," said Craz, who stayed behind to clean up the mess they'd made. The table was littered with balled-up sketches and several empty bags of barbecue chips that had fueled their creative session. Craz scooped up the mess and tossed everything into the garbage but stopped short when he heard a loud *thunk* of something obviously not paper landing in the metal basket.

"Uh-oh," he said as he immediately saw that he'd just thrown Matt's pen into the trash. *It must've been hiding under the scraps of paper,* Craz thought as he bent down to rescue it. He slid the pen into his pocket and then slung his backpack over his shoulder before leaving the library.

Craz headed down the hallway, where kids were busy trying to get out of school as fast as possible. Lockers were slamming shut. Kids were shouting to their friends. It was chaotic, and Craz liked the wild vibe. He passed Mrs. Bentz's classroom and saw his teacher bent over her desk, correcting a stack of papers with her nasty red pen. He stood by the door watching as she slashed and hacked at essays and then, with a chuckle, drew a huge *F* on the paper in front of her. She seemed to be enjoying herself too much, Craz thought before pulling the new cartoon out of his backpack and looking at it again. A sly grin spread on his face.

"Next stop," he said, staring at the cartoon, "Treasure Island."

27

AN ISLAND VACATION

FINALLY HOME AFTER A LONG SCHOOL DAY, Mrs. Bentz opened another can of cat food and dumped the smelly mess into the big bowl on the kitchen floor. "Okay, sweeties," she called. "Supper!"

Five cats of different shapes and sizes instantly swarmed her feet and started feasting on the gross-smelling pile of tuna Treat-Ums. Not counting her cats, Mrs. Bentz lived alone in a stucco apartment near the Laundromat. It was a neat one-bedroom home that she decorated with a collection of tiny ceramic statues of rosy-cheeked cherubs and a series of paintings all depicting summer, her favorite time of year. She loved her apartment, which was a tidy, immaculate space that made her feel calm after her long, thankless days teaching unruly adolescents.

After feeding her cats, Mrs. Bentz emerged into the living room looking like a psychedelic sausage in her Day-Glo spandex exercise clothes and thick terry-cloth headband. She turned on the TV, slid her favorite aerobics DVD into the player, and as the upbeat music began to fill the room, she started her workout while her five cats purred from their perches on the couch.

On the TV the perky instructor stepped from side to side, swinging her arms in wide circles. Mrs. Bentz followed along, looking far less graceful but ready for the burn. "Momma's gonna get in shape!" she shouted to the cats on the couch. "Just you watch!"

CRAZ ARRIVED AT COPY-COPY AND LEFT HIS bike outside while he went into the store with the new cartoon. He walked to the self-serve machine and was surprised to see an OUT OF ORDER sign there.

"What happened to the copier?" he asked Mr. Hupt, who, as usual, was bent over the larger machine in the back of the shop, banging on it with a wrench.

Mr. Hupt dropped the wrench and wiped his hands on his pants. He turned around. It was Boyd T. Boone. "Just a little paper jam," he said with the familiar twinkle in his eye. "Or a toner problem. Can I level with you? Don't know, don't care."

Craz was starting to get used to these sudden appearances by the cartoonist. The guy was weird. That was for sure. But Craz was still glad to see him again. "I just need to make a quick copy. Got some unfinished *teacher business* to deal with, if you know what I mean."

"I know exactly what you mean," Boyd T. Boone said with a broad wink. "Hand it over and we'll take care of it back here."

THE SWEAT WAS POURING OFF MRS. BENTZ AS she copied the dance moves on the DVD. "Gotta move it to lose it," she cried out as her heart beat like a sledgehammer in her chest. "Feel the burn, kitties!"

She was so used to feeling slightly light-headed and dizzy while she hit the hardest part of the workout that she hardly noticed the moment when her cozy living room disappeared and was replaced by lush, tropical island foliage.

"Hold on," she said, suddenly aware of a swarm of mosquitoes buzzing her sweaty head. She pressed her hand to her heart. "Am I having a stroke?"

The aerobics music was gone, replaced by the distant crash of waves and the sudden squawk of an unseen parrot shouting, "Pieces of eight, Capt'n. Pieces of eight!"

Completely confused, Mrs. Bentz took a few tentative steps toward the noise. Peering through some palm fronds, she saw a white sandy beach and five men who either were dressed for Halloween or were actual pirates.

Pirates!

She stared again and saw that the men had cutlasses and hooped earrings—and then she gasped. The one shouting orders leaned on a wooden crutch and had only one leg! Could it really be Long John Silver? In the flesh!

Mrs. Bentz strained to see the name of the massive boat anchored in the harbor.

"Oh, dear," she said, overwhelmed as the letters came into focus. *"Hispaniola!"*

Mrs. Bentz felt like she'd died and gone to heaven.

28

CARTOONIST CRAZ

CRAZ HAD NO IDEA IF THE MAGIC HAD WORKED, but he couldn't help smiling at the thought that his teacher was shipwrecked far, far away.

"So give me a coming attraction. Do I get a substitute teacher tomorrow?" he asked Boyd T. Boone, who was holding up the Treasure Island cartoon and the copied image like fresh fruit he'd just picked from a tree.

"Guess you'll have to wait and see," the cartoonist said as he handed the drawings back. "That's the way the cookies crumble." Boyd T. Boone then poked the corner of his mouth with his tongue. "Speaking of cookies, how about you draw me a nice bag of chocolate-pecan-chips?"

Craz laughed. "Actually, Matt's the cartoonist. I'm just the idea guy."

"*Just the idea guy!*" Boyd T. Boone stood up straight and placed his hands on his wide hips. "Don't sell yourself short, bucko. Cartoons without ideas are just lines," he said. "Besides, everyone is a cartoonist. Some just make better doodles than others." Boyd T. Boone leaned across the counter. "Don't tell me there isn't *anything* you'd want to draw right here, right now?"

"There's plenty I want, but trust me. I can't draw."

"Everyone can draw," Boyd T. Boone said. "With a little help."

Craz shook his head. "Not me. Even my stick people look messed up."

"Yeah. Drawing people can be tough," the cartoonist said. "But there are plenty of other things to draw. If you want to, that is."

Craz thought for a second, then looked out the door at his sad hand-me-down bike leaning against the parking meter. Besides all the rust, the brakes were shot and the tires were totally bare of tread. "I guess it would be nice to have a cool new bike. All I've ever had were used pieces of junk," he said, and sighed. "But I wouldn't have a clue how to draw one. Seriously."

"Hmm. I bet that's just years of nasty art teachers filling your head with nonsense." Boyd T. Boone flashed his toothy smile. "All you need to draw something is the *idea* of it . . . and you've got that base covered, right?"

Craz thought about Matt. He would definitely not be happy if Craz used the pen to draw something wild and potentially troublesome like a pocket-size time machine or a popcorn-popping robot that did your homework. Too many things could go wrong. But a new bike was pretty safe. It was just a simple object that he could really use.

Craz took a deep breath. "Why not? What do I have to lose?"

"That's the spirit!" Boyd T. Boone shouted.

Craz reached into his pocket and pulled out the pen. Sure, he'd signed his name with it before, but holding it now felt really different. For the first time he was about to use it to draw something, and that made all the difference.

"Um, where do I start?" he asked the cartoonist.

"You start by closing your eyes and picturing what

you want in your mind. And I mean really see it," Boyd T. Boone said.

Craz closed his eyes and tried to imagine the bike that he'd want.

"Oh, and while you're at it . . . ," Boyd T. Boone added. "Could you picture those cookies, too?"

MATT WAS DOING SOME MATH HOMEWORK WHEN the doorbell rang. He yelled twice for Ricky to answer it, but after the third ring he finally gave up and went to see who was being such a pain.

"Hello, Matt," Craz said, leaning casually against the door frame with his arms behind his back. "Wuzzup?"

Matt stared at his best friend. Craz was never very good at keeping secrets, and Matt could always tell if Craz was hiding something by the way he blinked too much. And right now his eyelids were a blur.

"What did you do?" Matt asked suspiciously.

"What did I do? I copied the Treasure Island cartoon," Craz answered. "Oh, and I got an iguana."

Craz pulled his hands out from his back and revealed a bright green foot-long lizard, who looked up at Matt and then tried to chew a button on his shirt sleeve. "His name is Virgil."

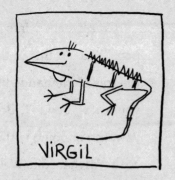

VIRGIL

"Craz," Matt began, his anger slowly boiling. "Since when do you have an iguana?"

"And a new bike!" Craz stepped aside so Matt could see the bicycle that he'd created—a sleek, silver fifteen-speed beauty with a dark leather seat, fat lime-green tires, and an iPod built into the handlebars.

"Pretty rockin', isn't it?"

Matt wasn't so sure. "But how did this happen? I didn't draw a bike, and I definitely didn't draw that thing!" Matt pointed at the iguana, who had climbed up Craz's arm and draped himself across Craz's head like some sort of living hat.

"Hey, you're not the only cartoonist, you know," Craz fumed. "I can draw too."

Matt walked down the steps to look closer at Craz's new bike. "I'm not saying you can't draw, Craz. I was just wondering *how* you drew all of this. We only have one pen."

Craz reached into his backpack and pulled out the pen. "You left this in the library. I almost chucked it into the trash." He handed the pen back to Matt. "And just so you know, Boyd. T. Boone says drawing is natural, like yawning or going to the bathroom. Anyone can do it, and so that's what I did. Well, actually, he helped me draw what I wanted by showing me what to do. But I held the pen!"

"Wait. You saw him again?"

"Yup. One minute I was talking to him at Copy-Copy, and the next minute old Mr. Hupt was giving me my change. Of course, I'd already made my copies, as you can plainly see."

Craz lifted Virgil from his head and shoved the iguana into Matt's face. "Cute, isn't he?"

Matt felt the scratchy lick from the iguana's tiny tongue and was thankful Craz hadn't wanted a pet horse. He then took a closer look at the bike. Craz had obviously gone all out with his drawing. Spring suspension. Shiny chrome gears. A fancy basket for carrying stuff. "Craz, what is this?" Matt asked, pointing to the strange thing added to the back of the bike that looked like a huge hair dryer.

"That, my friend, is a booster engine," Craz said proudly. "I was toying with retractable wings but went with the rocket instead. Way easier to draw. Nice touch, huh?"

"No. Not a nice touch," Matt snapped back. "What happened to keeping things below the radar? A new pet is one thing. I get it. But couldn't you just draw a *normal* bike instead of a souped-up rocket-powered one?"

"But it can achieve speeds of up to sixty miles per hour!" Craz held Virgil out by his side and zoomed him in a sweeping circle like an airplane. He sighed. "Fine. I got carried away.

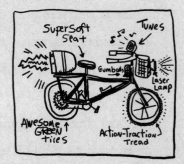

But I never knew drawing stuff was so fun. You just picture something, crank out a doodle, and then, ZAP, it's real."

"Real trouble," Matt said. "Let's put your bike in my garage before someone gets a close look at it and starts asking questions." Matt grabbed the bike and began wheeling it to the driveway.

Craz ran to catch up. "When did you get to be such a dud?"

"I'm not a dud," Matt said defensively. "I'm just a cautious guy."

Craz grabbed the bike from Matt. "Aren't you tired of being that guy?"

Matt had to admit that he hated always being afraid. Just once he wished he was more like Craz and could be the one who would grab the bike and feel the wind rush past him as he wildly zoomed around his quiet neighborhood, outracing the crazed dogs who loved to chase anything that moved.

"Tell you what," said Craz. "Let me be the 'cautious guy' so you don't have to be." He balanced Virgil on his shoulder and handed the bike helmet to Matt. Then he dramatically wrung his hands together, acting like he was nervous. "I don't think it's a good idea to try out my new bike, Matt. Don't do it! Something terrible might happen."

Matt had to laugh. "That's what I sound like?" he said. "Oh, man. I am a dud." Matt took a deep breath, then cautiously put the helmet on and swung his leg over the middle post so he was straddling Craz's bike. He could do this. Going for a ride would be fun. "But for the record, I don't whine like that."

Craz smiled as he turned on the iPod and cranked the music. The tiny speakers embedded in the handlebars blasted tunes back into Matt's face.

"Nice touch with the speakers," Matt said over the music.

"Thanks," said Craz. "FYI, the brakes are perfectly adjusted, so no sudden stops or you might flip over the handlebars, okay?"

"Right," said Matt as he pumped the brakes to feel how tight they were. "No sudden stops."

"And when you're ready for the booster, just flip this switch." Craz showed Matt a red toggle switch that was located above the water bottle. "Then hang on. You're going to freak out at how fast you'll go! Your face muscles are going to actually hurt!"

Matt felt his heart pumping. He couldn't believe he was actually going through with something so wild. He tried to imagine how the rocket-powered ride was going to feel. The speed. The freedom. The wind in his face. It was exciting. It was dangerous.

His stomach dropped.

It *was* dangerous, which meant that instead of the

wind in his hair, he pictured the scars across his face, the ambulance ride to the hospital, the metal pins that would have to be inserted into his legs.

He got off the bike. "I can't," was all he said as he handed the helmet back to Craz and walked, defeated, to his house.

"What happened?" yelled Craz.

Matt sighed. "I'm just not you," he said before letting the screen door slam shut behind him.

Craz stood on the front steps staring at the closed door. Matt was obviously feeling bad, which was why Craz decided not to tell his friend about the other cartoon that he had drawn and copied.

Craz took the folded-up paper from his back pocket and looked at it again and smiled. It wasn't a great piece of art, but it didn't have to be. It just had to give him what he'd always wanted.

"See that?" he said to Virgil, who sat comfortably in the bike's front basket. "I'm not just the idea guy." And then he put the drawing back into his pocket, jumped onto his bike, and rocketed away down the street, leaving a cloud of dust behind him.

29

CRAZ'S NEW LIFE

WALKING INTO HIS HOUSE, CRAZ INSTANTLY
knew something was different. First, instead of the usual
obstacle course of mud-covered sneakers and carelessly
kicked-off shoes waiting to trip him in the hallway, there
was just one set of ladies' rain boots carefully placed
on the floor and a pair of men's running shoes lined up,
neat and tidy, by the door. He kicked his sneakers off and
watched them land haphazardly on the tiles, not caring
that they looked so messy next to the other two pairs.

"I'm home," he hollered as he tossed his hooded
sweatshirt onto the stairway banister—and then did a
double take because the wooden railing was completely

clear of the mishmash mess of jackets and sweaters that were usually draped there.

And it was quiet. *Really* quiet.

He was careful to keep Virgil hidden inside his jacket as he walked through the dining room, which was also strangely clutter-free. He stepped into the kitchen, where his mother should have been frantically throwing together some sort of disgusting dinner that would feed all seven Crazinskis.

"Hi, honey. How was your day?" Craz's mother sat at the clean kitchen table, where she calmly sipped mint tea while reading some sort of fashion magazine.

"My day was…interesting," Craz responded, surprised to see that his mother wasn't running around the kitchen. He'd also never seen her read any magazines except waiting in line with an overflowing shopping cart at the supermarket. And that was so she could wipe her wrists on the free perfume sample pages.

Craz caught a whiff of something cooking. It was a smell he didn't know because it actually smelled good. "What's for supper? Did you order takeout?"

His mother put the magazine down and smiled. She usually looked like she'd slapped on her makeup and combed her hair with a fork. But now her hair was brushed and stylish, and she looked actually pretty. His mom? Pretty? How weird.

"Dinner tonight is your favorites," she said. "Risotto with mushrooms. Spinach mini-quiche. And for dessert, flourless chocolate cake."

Craz had no idea what risotto was, and besides the chocolate cake, which actually sounded edible, the rest of the menu didn't sound anything like the usual pot of spaghetti and bowl of tossed salad. Fancy food had never been on the menu before. Not in his house.

"No offense, Mom, but when did you learn to cook?"

His mother looked up and laughed. "Larry, you kidder, you." She waved her hand at him, a gesture that showed off her painted nails, which was another thing that stuck out like a pimple on a cheerleader.

"Uh, I'm going to be in my room," Craz said, backing out of the kitchen while keeping an eye on his mother. Maybe it was just some big act she was putting on. Or maybe she had been watching one of those dumb makeover shows on TV, and that's why the food was so bizarre and the house felt so clean.

Upstairs he walked past his sisters' bedroom, and then froze in his tracks. He backed up and stared into the room, which was no longer crowded with the two single beds, a large wooden dollhouse, a messy paper-covered desk, and a closet overflowing with clothes.

"Sweet," Craz said, standing in front of a fifty-five-inch flat-screen TV that took up most of one wall. He hadn't known his parents were going to turn Meagan and Becca's room into an entertainment center. He showed the room to his iguana. "Look, Virgil! My sisters don't have a room anymore," Craz said while he stretched out on the long, soft couch that sat opposite the TV. He quickly flipped through the channels until he found a cool-looking volcano documentary. With a TV that big the bright red lava was practically flowing onto his lap. "I can get used to this!"

And then it hit him.

His sisters didn't have a bedroom. The house was quiet and clean. His mother had painted her fingernails!

Craz ran to the bathroom. No mountain of dirty

towels. No assortment of shampoos scattered along the bathtub wall. And there were only three toothbrushes in the plastic cup on the sink.

He rummaged through his backpack to grab the cartoon he'd made. All he'd wanted was to be able to take a long, hot shower. If he didn't have sisters or brothers, then he could shower for as long as he wanted. Had he accidentally used the pen to make himself an only child?

He raced to his own bedroom, which was no less of a surprise. Instead of his brothers' bunk beds and the tiny single bed that he slept on, one big double-size bed took up most of the room. That would be *his* bed. All his! He looked around the room.

The closet had only his clothes.

The bookshelf held only his books.

And the incredibly slow computer that Hank had rebuilt with used parts and a really old CPU had been replaced with a snazzy fast PC that had a monitor twice the size of his old one. And this computer was his and his alone!

He felt bad about his siblings, but come on. . . . Look at all this great stuff!

He turned on the new sound system and cranked his music. At least his playlists were still the same. He danced around his room, abandoning all thoughts of the huge family that he'd had to share everything with. More people obviously meant less stuff. Now the house was filled with cool new things, and Craz liked it, even if it meant eating something called risotto.

As the music blared, he held Virgil to his chest and fell backward onto his huge bed, feeling for the first time ever that his family was finally perfect.

30

FAMILY DINNER

CASA CUBANA HAD THE BEST GRILLED CHICKEN on the planet. Large pieces of garlic stuck out from under crispy brown skin, and each plate came with a pile of rice, black beans, and soft, yummy plantains. The restaurant wasn't fancy. The place was located in a strip mall stuffed between a party supply store and a barbershop. From the outside it looked like just another dump. But inside it came alive with a variety of different-size tables—all with mismatched chairs, multicolored lightbulbs draped over the bar, and bouncy Cuban music playing in the background.

"I've missed this place," Matt said as he drained his second root beer. He especially liked the old glass soda bottles. "We haven't eaten here in, like, forever."

"What are you talking about?" Matt's mom asked while she popped a piece of garlic-soaked bread into her mouth. "We come here every week."

"That's right. It's Monday night, so that means the Worfles go to Casa Cubana." Matt's dad sat across the table, holding hands with his mom. "Nothing better than family traditions, right?"

Of course. Matt had forgotten that, thanks to his cartoon, his father had never moved out. So to Matt, being all together again felt new, but to the rest of his family, nothing had changed . . . except that his parents were actually getting along great.

"So, Ricky. I've been thinking. How about you and I head down to McMaster's this weekend. Pick you out a nice six-stringer? Maybe even an amp."

Ricky dropped his fork. "A guitar? You mean it?"

Matt was just as shocked. He hadn't drawn this part, and he definitely hadn't drawn his mother's reaction.

"David, I thought we'd agreed that Ricky needed to do a little better in school first." Her voice stayed calm, but she looked pretty mad. "It's a decision we should make together."

Mr. Worfle laughed. "What's the big deal? Let the kid have a little fun while he's working on his grades. Nothing wrong with fun, right?"

"I'm with Dad. Fun is good," Ricky said, smiling for the first time all night. "You're the best, Dad."

"And, Matt, I think a trip to Easel & Brush might be a good idea too. What do you say? Colored pencils? Some fancy paper? Whatever you want!"

The waiter placed a new bottle of root beer in front of Matt, who poured out a frothy glassful while he searched his mother's face for her reaction. She was staring at her dinner, and Matt could tell something was bothering her.

"Well?" his dad asked. "What do you think, sport? New art stuff?"

"Sure. Sounds great to me, Dad!" Matt clinked glasses with his father.

"I know you're still eating, but make sure to save room for dessert," the waiter said. "We have flan tonight. And you know how fast it disappears."

"Count me in," Mr. Worfle said as he patted his stomach. "How about you, Mindy?"

Still a little mad, Matt's mom finally smiled. She couldn't resist the dessert. "Save one for me, Juan Carlos. I can't come here and not have the flan."

Ricky had already put his headphones back on, so they just went ahead and ordered him one. "What about you, Matt? Dessert?"

"Are you kidding?" Matt looked up at the waiter, and his mouth fell open. "Dessert . . ."

"Yes. Warm flan. Just for you." The waiter was grinning like an idiot. An idiot who was Boyd T. Boone.

"Yeah, sure . . . ," Matt said, still staring at the waiter. "Whatever this guy says goes."

"*Muy bien,*" Boyd T. Boone replied with a flash of his grin. "Flan for the *happy* family."

CRAZ TENTATIVELY POKED HIS FORK INTO THE mound of risotto on his plate. "You say I actually eat this stuff? It looks like rice. Rice looks like maggots. I hate rice."

"You love rice," Mr. Crazinski corrected him from across the dining room table. "And since when do you hate your mother's risotto? You usually inhale it."

So this is what happens when you change your family, Craz thought. Your taste buds just kind of go along for the ride.

Craz lifted a forkful to his mouth and let the fluffy risotto sit on his tongue. He chewed. The texture was kind of mushy, but his father was right—he did like it. He started shoveling the stuff in.

"So tell us, Larry. What did you learn in school today?" His mother put her hands together and rested her chin on the tips of her fingers. She stared at him with a smile, waiting for him to speak.

Craz looked up and saw both his parents watching him, waiting for him to answer. He could hear the faint ticking of his father's watch and wished someone else would pick up the conversation slack or start arguing about something stupid, but he realized he was the only other one there. It was all up to him.

"Today, huh?" he stalled, running the school day through his brain. "Um, let's see. Oh, right. There was a pep rally. That was a total waste of time."

Craz assumed he was done and took a bite of the spinach mini-quiche on his plate. *Not bad,* he thought. Maybe this version of his mom was on to something.

His father cleared his throat. His smile had faded into a tight-lipped scowl. "But what did you *learn* today, Son? That's why you go to school. To learn."

Normally Craz would skip over this kind of question by kicking any of his siblings under the table. The fight that would erupt would take over and simply derail any and all topics. He looked at his dad's face again. He meant business.

"Okay." Craz racked his brain for some sort of fun factoid. "Did you know that kids my age are full of hormones? And there's this gland thing . . . the, uh, sea biscuit gland—"

"Sebaceous gland," corrected his father.

"Right, the sebaceous gland, which churns out all this oil, which can build up and make zits."

He stopped, hoping he was done with the talking thing, but his parents just stared at him, wanting more.

"What else did you learn today?" Craz's father asked

as he dabbed at the corner of his mouth and then patiently folded his napkin.

"And don't leave out a single thing." His mother clicked her perfect fingernails together like bright red candies.

Craz was not used to dinner being so much work. All he wanted to do was eat. But it was obvious that his parents really did want to know about his day. And when was the last time his mom and dad had given him this kind of undivided attention?

"Hold on," Craz said, and then he jammed his mouth with risotto and a big bite of quiche. He chewed the mixture quickly, swallowed, and then told his parents every detail about his school day . . . except the part about Mrs. Bentz and the cartoon that had hopefully given her an unexpected island vacation.

That detail was better off kept a secret.

31

SNORE-FEST

CINDY OCKABLOOM HAD RUN FOR STUDENT council because she thought it would be fun to meet new kids. That was the good part of junior high school, getting exposed to brand-new sets of people who had the potential to make your life either better or worse.

For Matt and Craz those results had been pretty terrible, mostly because they had come up against snarky jerks like Skip Turkle and Diesel McKenzie. Cindy, on the other hand, was doing just fine, and after winning over all sorts of kids she'd never known before, she was easily elected the school's new treasurer.

The elections had been a week ago, and today was the day the new student council got to address the whole school in what promised to be the most boring assembly ever. The four elected council members—Marcia Liddle, president; Gary Needleman, vice president; Tommy Pierpont, secretary; and Cindy Ockabloom, treasurer—were seated in a neat row on the stage in front of the purple velvet curtain emblazoned with a large Kilgore Killer Bee.

Principal Droon was banging on the microphone, trying to get the auditorium to quiet down. "Please, let's keep the chatter to a minimum. I know you're all excited to meet your Kilgore student council."

Paulie Frick snored loudly, and his jock friends all laughed.

Principal Droon gave Paulie the evil eyeball and then continued. "And just a reminder that our fall parent-teacher meetings are tonight. Six p.m. sharp, people. I expect to see you all on your best behaviors. Your parents, too!"

"Ugh, I hate when my parents and teachers mix," Matt said, sinking lower into his seat. "It's like two opposite worlds colliding and I'm in the middle of the explosion."

"I dunno. I have a good feeling about tonight." Craz grinned, imagining that his new family situation was going to make this parent-teacher meeting great. "I actually can't wait."

Principal Droon took his seat on the metal folding chair next to the flag, which gave Marcia Liddle the chance to finally address the student body.

This shouldn't be too painful, Matt thought, happy to have the perfect excuse to stare at Cindy, who looked incredible, as always. He took out the new pen and did a few little doodles of her to pass the time.

"Thank you for your confidence, Kilgore Junior High!" Marcia, a pencil-thin girl whose hair resembled a poorly made black scrub brush, yelled into the microphone at the lectern. She pounded her fist. "Changes are afoot, fellow students. The cafeteria has promised me that they will rename American chop suey 'macaroni and meat sauce' so as not to offend any of our socially sensitive students." She waited for the roar of approval that never came, and then pushed on. "Remember your new student council is leading the way!"

Marcia motioned to Tommy, Gary, and Cindy, who

waved to the audience while Principal Droon clapped wildly, looking like a sappy seal.

"Hey, I'm sorry if I made you mad yesterday," Craz said quietly to Matt. "And just so you know, I left the rocket bike at home. And I've got Virgil hidden in my room." He didn't mention his new econo-size family. That detail he kept to himself.

Matt sighed. "You didn't do anything wrong. I'm just a wimp."

"Come on, that booster engine was a wacko idea. Totally nuts!"

"Maybe." Matt looked at his friend. "But I could've at least *tried* riding the bike. Even a little."

Onstage Marcia continued reading from her note cards, proposing that the janitors start using pine-scented toilet bowl cleaner and put goat's milk hand soap in all the bathrooms.

"You want to know the truth?" said Craz. "I didn't even use the bike's booster."

"Really?" asked Matt.

Craz couldn't help but grin. "Are you kidding? I raced

that baby all the way home! It was sick." He paused.
"But seriously? You totally did the right thing. That bike
would've killed you."

Matt looked down at the scuffed-up floor. "Thanks. I
think."

Craz could tell that Matt was upset. "Look, Matt, you
didn't go for it. I totally admire that. You actually know
what works for you and what doesn't. Me? There's no
pause button. I say yes to stuff before even knowing

what it is I agree to do." Craz waited for Matt to look back up at him. "I know you wish you were different. . . . Well, me too. Really."

Matt finally spoke. "You *can* be a total goof sometimes."

"No doubt," Craz said, then smiled. "At least I'm good at something."

The bell rang finally, putting an end to the assembly. Marcia tried to get the students to join in on a song she'd written, but kids fled their seats, glad to be getting the blood circulating in their numb butts.

"TALK ABOUT DEATH-DEFYING," DIESEL McKENZIE said as he filed out of the auditorium. "I think I dozed off back there. Twice!"

"I don't get it," said Skip Turkle as he pushed past the clog of smaller kids in his way. "Why would anyone actually want to be on student council?"

"Aliens," Diesel said. "Like they're from another planet."

"Another planet. Good one." Skip snorted. He stopped in the middle of the hallway and grabbed Diesel's short shoulder. "Hey, what time you got?"

Diesel checked his watch. "One o'clock. Why?"

The wheels were spinning in Skip's head. He had an idea. "Tuesday's *Lantern* doesn't get printed for another hour. You up for making a last-minute editorial cartoon?"

Diesel grinned. "Oh, yeah."

32

CRASH COURSE

CRAZ HAD TO MAKE A PIT STOP BEFORE THE next period, so he took off for the nearest bathroom, which gave Matt a good excuse to casually hang around the water fountain that just happened to be next to Cindy's locker. He wasn't sure if he'd actually be able to speak to her, but the thought of possibly getting a whiff of her shampoo made him feel that the risk was worth taking.

He was drinking a nice, long sip of water when he heard Cindy's voice.

"I thought Marcia did an amazing job up there," she was saying. "Though, I think her idea to create retina-scan ID checkpoints is a bit over the top."

Matt looked up and saw Cindy walking straight toward him with her friend Geena. He tried to swallow the water in his mouth, but it all went down the wrong way and he choked and started coughing in loud, wheezing gasps.

"Oof! Ergh! Ack!"

Bent over and hacking, Matt backed away from the water fountain just as Diesel and Skip rounded the corner on their way to the stairway. They were in a rush to get to the *Lantern* office and so didn't notice Matt stumble into their path, and he was too busy trying to get oxygen into his lungs to see the terrible twosome barreling his way.

"Look out!" yelled Cindy just as Skip and Diesel rammed into Matt, sending three sets of books and papers into the air.

Matt and Diesel ended up on the floor as the snowstorm of paper came down on top of them. Skip, thanks to his low center of gravity, remained upright just fine.

"You idiot!" yelled Diesel. "Walk much?"

Matt was just about to say something when a miracle happened. Cindy Ockabloom put out her perfect

hand and reached down to help Matt up. "I saw the whole thing. They crashed into you, Matt."

Matt was dazed. He reached for Cindy's hand, but all he could think was, *Cindy Ockabloom said my name!*

He let her help him to his feet. "Thanks," he said out loud while tiny voices in his head were shouting, *You did it! You talked to her!*

Matt let Cindy's shampoo smell surround him. Strawberry. He had never been happier.

"Hey, Worfle," Diesel piped up from the floor. "You think you can help sort through this mess you made? I've got places to be."

"And things to do," added Skip, who, unwilling to bend down, was using his sneaker to round up stray objects that might be his.

Matt looked at Cindy. She was smiling. He smiled back. "I better, you know . . . do this."

"Good idea," Cindy said. "It was nice seeing you."

"It was?" Matt knew instantly that he shouldn't have said something stupid like that. But it was too late. Cindy was already back at her locker. The moment, all twenty-eight seconds, had come and gone.

Matt got down on his knees and reached for his green three-ring notebook, while Diesel was working, ferret-like, to make little piles of his own stuff.

"This is my math book . . . my binder . . . my science report." Diesel moved quickly, shuffling through the jumble of objects. He grabbed a thick book, flipped through its pages, and then slid it across the floor to Matt like a hockey puck. "That's definitely your copy of *Treasure Island*, Worfle. Mine is full of useful notes."

Treasure Island. Between the brain-numbing assembly and his moment of happiness with Cindy, Matt had forgotten all about the cartoon he and Craz had made.

Had it worked? Was Mrs. Bentz actually marooned in a book?

The bell rang. Matt grabbed at his loose pencils and pens and quickly shoved them into his backpack. He had to get to English.

"Aren't you guys coming to class?" Matt asked as he stood back up.

"Nope. We've got important stuff to do," said Skip. *"Newspaper stuff."*

Diesel rounded up his remaining papers, a dog-eared science book, and a couple of pens, which he absently slid into his pocket. "That's what happens when you're important, Worfle. You get to miss classes, and teachers don't mind. Not that you'd know anything about that!"

Diesel and Skip hurried off toward the stairs that led to the *Lantern* office as Matt walked down the hall, following the lingering scent of Cindy's shampoo. As the late bell rang, he actually ran for class, anxious to meet up with Craz and find out what, if anything, had happened to Mrs. Bentz.

33

MEANWHILE . . .

"HEAVE HO!" SHOUTED THE SUN-SOAKED PIRATE,
who went by the name of Job Anderson. "Just cuz you're
womanly don't make no bones with me. Shoulder those
oars!"

Mrs. Bentz was helping the pirates carry their jolly-
boat from the beach into the jungle. It was hot, sweaty
work, and she couldn't be happier.

"So tell me again," the one-legged Long John Silver
said as he hobbled behind the crew. "You say you're from
the future?"

"From the future!" squawked Captain Flint, the parrot
perched on Long John's shoulder.

"Well, technically, it's the present," Mrs. Bentz said,

as more sweat dripped off her headband and into her eyes. This was a way better workout than her silly step aerobics DVD. "See, you're all characters in a book. And I'm having some sort of wildly vivid dream."

"Aye, so we're all in this dream of yours, are we?" Long John arched an eyebrow as he stopped to lean on his crutch and take a long draw on his pipe.

"That's the only explanation," Mrs. Bentz said with a grunt. "But for the life of me I don't remember going to sleep."

Dick Johnson, a third pirate, leaned over so he could talk softly to his one-legged leader. "I think this one has been in the sun too long, I do. And look at what be her garb."

Both pirates eyed Mrs. Bentz, who remained stuffed into her two-piece fluorescent workout clothes.

"A more feverish guise I've never seen. Should we cut her free of her demons?" And with this, Dick lifted his cutlass as a threat.

"I say not," Long John Silver whispered back. "Odd as she be, she may just help us with that heavy promise of treasure that's waitin' ahead. Of course, once we're loaded up and the gold is ours to keep, there's no tellin' what might happen to her."

He smiled an evil grin and poked his calloused finger into Dick's gut.

"No tellin' at all. . . ."

34

SUBSTITUTE TEACHER

CRAZ WAS ALREADY SEATED BY THE TIME MATT got to class, anxious at the sight of their teacherless classroom.

"Bentz hasn't shown up yet," Craz said as Matt slid behind his desk. "Could be a good sign."

"Let's hope," said Matt. "Hey, guess who I actually spoke to?" A big grin was plastered on his face.

Craz had seen his friend's dopey look before. "Cindy? No way!"

"Oh, yeah," Matt said. "And she actually spoke back to me. It was almost a real conversation."

"Way to go, bro." Craz gave Matt a slap on the back.

"So, did you ask her out? Get her phone number? Make a plan?"

"Craz. I *talked* to her. Let's not rush into anything crazy, okay?"

"Fine. Just don't go all slo-mo on her. Seize the moment. We graduate in four years."

"I promise I'll keep the ball rolling. I mean, now that I've broken the ice, there's no telling what might happen, right?"

Craz smiled. "Right."

The door burst open and a large man wearing a black beret and huge sunglasses strode into the room. "Class, close your books and open your minds. Dull thinking will not be tolerated!"

Boyd T. Boone dropped a battered leather briefcase onto the floor. He opened it and took out a ham sandwich and a human skull, which he placed on the desk facing the kids. "Alas, poor Yorick. He flunked my class."

Matt and Craz high-fived. Their plan had obviously worked.

* * *

INSIDE THE *LANTERN* OFFICE, SKIP SAT WITH HIS
feet on his desk while he watched Diesel work fever-
ishly to get a last-minute cartoon into that day's paper.

"The Kilgore student council as aliens. I love it," Diesel
said as he penciled a rough sketch that made each of the
student council members into bizarre beings from outer
space. "You heard them at the assembly. It's like they just
want to take over the school. Totally from another planet."

Skip had a box of chocolates balanced on his legs.
He popped a dark chocolate caramel into his mouth.
"I know. All that yabbering on like they could actually
make this school a better place. Hogwash."

Diesel stopped drawing. "Wait. Did you really say,
'hogwash'?"

"I crack myself up sometimes," Skip said. "Hey, I

know. Hogwash should be their home planet! What do you think?"

In answer Diesel sketched a speech balloon above his alien characters and lettered the silly word as if they were all yelling it at once. "Perfect," he said, and then showed his finished draft to Skip.

Skip nodded. "As soon as you scan that cartoon, I've got it set up so the new issue will start printing. Hogwash and all." He popped another candy into his mouth. "How much time do you need to ink it up?"

Diesel rifled through his backpack. He pulled out his favorite eraser and a bunch of different pens. "Not much. Ten minutes. Max."

Skip used his pinky fingernail to dig out a chunk of caramel from one of his molars. "I love my job."

"Ditto," said Diesel. "Nothing better than making cartoons!" He spread his pens out on the desk and was looking for his favorite one, a Flexo-graph stylus with a .05-millimeter tip, when he noticed the strange green pen in his pile. He'd never seen the fancy pen before and figured that he must've picked it up after bumping into stupid Matt Worfle in the hallway. Diesel grinned, knowing Matt would most likely think he'd lost his pen.

Diesel uncapped his Flexo-graph pen but stopped. There was something about Matt's pen that made him curious. He picked it up and unscrewed the cap, testing how it felt in his hand. He inspected the shiny tip and then drew a few squiggly lines on a scrap of paper. He watched the ink flow and liked the fluid lines the pen made, which is why he scrapped his favorite pen for Matt's.

"Tough break, Worfle," he said, holding the ornate pen in his tiny hand.

Diesel blew across the alien drawing to clear off any dust. Then, using Matt's pen, he carefully inked over his pencil lines, having no idea he was making the last cartoon of his short career.

35

AFTER-SCHOOL SNACK

IT HAD BEEN A GOOD DAY. THEY'D GOTTEN TO miss health class because of the student council assembly, and then English had been a hoot with Boyd T. Boone as substitute teacher. He'd performed a one-man mash-up, mixing Hamlet with SpongeBob SquarePants. Totally wild.

To celebrate, Matt invited Len and Sammy to join him and Craz for a pig-out at the Shack. Their treat. After all, they'd used the pen to make some more money, and what good is having free cash if you don't share it with your friends?

"I hope Bentz is on a nice long vacation," said Len as they walked down Main Street. "That sub guy is awesome."

"And let's be honest," added Sammy. "How great was it getting a break from *Treasure Island*? I forgot English could actually be cool." Sammy opened the door, and the guys walked into the Shack, instantly inhaling the scent of greasy french fries and burgers.

"Ahh, heaven," sighed Matt. "Hey, where's Hank? Day off?"

Craz's first reaction was to look around for his brother, but then he remembered Hank didn't work there because Hank didn't exist. He didn't have any brothers. Or sisters. And for half a second Craz's stomach twisted into a little knot.

"Right," Craz said with a nervous chuckle. "Hank's got the day off." Craz quickly looked away and led the guys to a corner booth.

It was decided that four orders of fries and a milk shake apiece should start them off just fine. While they devoured their snacks, the conversation turned to their favorite nonschool topic: girls.

"Nancy Applebaum. Now, there's a girl I could get crazy about," Sammy said. "Smart. Cute. And she hasn't hit her growth spurt yet, so I'm still taller than her."

"She's definitely in your height range," said Craz. "Of course, you have a better chance of discovering a fifth dimension than going out with her."

The guys laughed, and even Sammy had to agree. Nancy's orbit was nowhere near his.

"Hey, speaking of impossible matchups," Craz said. "Guess who Mr. Matt finally got chatty with."

"Cindy?" Sammy was shocked. "No way . . ."

Matt grinned. "Yup. And you know what? Once I actually said a few words, talking to her was easy. Sort of."

"I knew you could do it," said Len, raising his glass. "That's what I've been talking about!"

Sammy took a long swig of his milk shake. "So, what did you think of that editorial cartoon of Cindy in today's *Lantern*? Pretty funny, right?"

"You know we don't read that trash," Craz coolly said.

But Matt was curious. "What cartoon?"

Sammy reached into his backpack and pulled out a folded copy of the newspaper, which had been distributed around the school during last period. "Diesel made all the student council members into aliens. It's actually pretty good."

Matt grabbed the newspaper and flipped through the pages until he found Diesel's half-page cartoon. Sure enough, there were the four student council kids made into four different alien creatures. The big-headed, oval-eyed leader was clearly meant to be Marcia, and she was holding a scepter that was shooting crazy blobs of goo. The other aliens wore name tags and were all yelling the same word—"hogwash." Matt searched the comic and saw that Diesel had drawn Cindy as a gelatinous blob with three eyeballs and a crooked smile.

Matt seethed any time he saw Diesel's byline in the *Lantern*, but this time it made him even madder

because the squirt had made fun of the girl he liked so much.

"I wish just once he'd use his pen to draw something that was actually funny." Matt balled up the newspaper and shoved it aside.

"I dunno. I thought it was kind of funny," offered Sammy. "I mean, not like your cartoons, Matt. But still..."

Craz changed the mood by ordering a second round of milk shakes and four brownie sundaes. Matt checked his wallet. He only had fifteen dollars left, which he knew wouldn't be enough.

"Uh, sorry, guys," Matt said. "But I don't think we can cover more snacks."

"What? Of course we can," butted in Craz. "We can always find some more money. Right, Matt?"

Matt's ears burned. He didn't like showing off their secret cash supply.

"How'd you guys get so loaded, anyway?" asked Len. "Did you score part-time jobs or something?"

"Long story," said Craz with a wink to Matt. "Let's just say we've been drawing the money from a secret account."

"Very secret," Matt added coldly as he jabbed an elbow into Craz's gut.

Craz leaned over to Matt and whispered, "Just slip outside, doodle up a few twenties, and zip over to Copy-Copy. Problem solved."

Matt stayed tight-lipped. "I just don't think we should solve every problem with the pen."

"It's your call," Craz said. "But the bill is going to come and we aren't going to be able to pay it. If you have another solution, I'm all ears."

"Fine!" Matt reached into his backpack and rummaged around for the pen. "That's weird," Matt said with his arm buried in his books and papers. "I can't find my pen."

"Here. Borrow mine," said Len, who held out a plastic ballpoint that he kept in his shirt pocket. "It's got a gel tip."

Matt started to freak. He dumped his entire backpack onto the table. Books spilled out onto the dirty dishes, along with sheets of loose paper, a few chewed-on pencils, and a long-forgotten rotted apple core. But no green pen. "It's not here!"

Craz tried to calm his friend down. "Maybe you left it at home."

"No. I had it at school. I know it."

"Okay. Think backward. When did you last see the pen?"

Matt bit his lower lip. "I had it at the assembly . . . and then . . ." Matt's eyes widened. "Oh, no."

Craz didn't like the look on Matt's face. "What is it?"

"I must've dropped it when Diesel and Skip crashed into me." Matt grabbed the balled-up newspaper and opened it to the alien cartoon. "And Diesel picked it up."

Now Craz shared Matt's horrified look. "You don't think he used it?"

Matt didn't bother to answer. He stuffed everything back into his backpack, grabbed his coat, and raced out the door. Craz wasted no time and quickly followed, leaving Len and Sammy clueless in the booth.

Len sighed. "Well, looks like we're buying our own snacks."

36

OOZE NEWS

DIESEL AND SKIP WERE SUSPENDED INSIDE A bright green gelatinous bubble. It was entirely Diesel's fault too. If he hadn't added the ornate scepter to his cartoon, then the alien version of Marcia wouldn't have had the power to enslave anyone with her intergalactic goo. But hindsight is twenty-twenty and unfortunately, as soon as Diesel had finished the comic, Skip had made a scan of it, which had brought the quartet of student council aliens into the *Lantern* office.

"*Gorgle-hack!*" the Marcia alien had shouted.

"Hogwash!" the other three had screeched.

Diesel had stared openmouthed at the creatures that looked remarkably like his cartoon, while Skip had protected his box of chocolates from the aliens' prying eyes. And then Marcia raised her scepter and aimed it at the two boys, instantly capturing them (and the chocolates) in the blob of green translucent slime.

BY THE TIME MATT AND CRAZ GOT BACK TO school, the only other kids still hanging around were the football players, who were having a late afternoon practice out on the field. As usual, Coach Arakanian was using his favorite motivation technique—screaming his head off. "You call those squats?" he shouted at the exhausted players. "You all disgust me. Twenty laps. NOW!"

Matt and Craz raced across the field, dodging the sweaty football players. They knew that in two hours the school would be swarming with parents and teachers, and the last thing anyone needed was to throw a bunch of aliens into the mix.

"Look. We aren't even sure if Diesel used the pen," said Craz. "Let's not go all worrywart over this. The best thing to do is—"

An eerie green glow suddenly lit up the *Lantern*'s basement windows, stopping Craz midsentence. "Never mind," he added. "C'mon!"

They rushed to the side of the school, and their worst fears were confirmed as soon as they knelt down and looked into the window.

There were the four aliens standing next to the prison of green slime. Diesel had really geeked out drawing Gary, who loomed over the others in excruciating detail, looking like a cross between a giant muscled cockroach and a slimy alien crab. The three-eyed undulating purple shape that was oozing all over Skip's desk was definitely Cindy, while Tommy rolled around in circles as an intergalactic robot with retractable tentacle arms. And Marcia, student council president and obvious leader of the group, stood proudly by them all, her huge almond eyes glowing brightly as her yellow reptilian skin reflected the glare of the fluorescent lights.

"For the record," Matt said, "I still hate Diesel's drawing style."

"But on the bright side," offered Craz, "Diesel and Skip look like they're stuck in my grandma's lime Jell-O mold!"

True. Diesel and Skip seemed totally helpless. If nothing else, Craz and Matt were happy about that. They were also happy to see the pen clutched in Diesel's fist . . . in the middle of the gross green goop.

"Okay. We just need to get our hands on the pen," said Craz. "Then you can doodle your way out of this. Agreed?"

"Agreed," Matt said. He looked at Cindy and sighed. Sure, she was a purple three-eyed alien, but she was still the cutest alien he'd ever seen.

37

DISTRACTIONS

THEIR PLAN SEEMED SIMPLE ENOUGH. CRAZ WOULD
create a diversion and Matt would rescue the pen.

"How hard could it be to get four aliens to chase me?"
Craz stood outside the *Lantern* office doing deep knee
bends and jumping jacks. "Ask anyone. I'm a natural
target."

He held the lid from a garbage can in one hand like a
shield. "You ready?"

"Ready," Matt lied. He hid behind the water fountain
and gave his friend a thumbs-up sign.

Craz sucked in his gut and then threw the *Lantern*
door open and leaped into the room. Surprised, all four
aliens immediately turned toward him.

The stench of alien BO hit him hard. "Whoa. Someone needs to hit the showers," Craz said with a pinched nose. "And, Gary, way to rock that creepy eye-twitch thing."

The giant cockroach alien bared his pointy teeth and hissed, ready to pounce. But Marcia held up a hand to keep Gary in line. Then her eyes narrowed as she raised her scepter and aimed it at Craz.

SPLOOSH! A blob of green goo shot straight at him.

"Ninja instincts!" Craz shouted as he quickly lifted the garbage can lid and blocked the ooze, spraying a splatter of the stuff all around him.

"You want to play that way?" he shouted before grabbing the fire extinguisher off the wall. "Eat my foam!"

Craz sprayed the room wildly, not even aiming. He just needed to make the aliens angry enough to chase him, and judging from the way the four started moving toward him, he thought he'd done a pretty good job.

Matt watched Craz bolt from the office with the four different-size aliens on his tail. He took a deep breath. Now it was up to him, and even though all he wanted to do was take off in the other direction, he forced himself to walk into the *Lantern* office.

"Whoa," Matt said, staring at the monstrous pile of green, which looked like something a huge alien dog might leave behind.

He hated to admit it but he really did enjoy seeing Skip and Diesel looking so scared. Up close Diesel's weasel eyes blinked repeatedly, a silent plea for help. In contrast Skip just looked annoyed, probably because a piece of chocolate was suspended just inches from his mouth and it was obviously driving him crazy.

Matt poked the blob with his finger. The stuff was icy cold to the touch and disgustingly thick, like cafeteria pudding. Getting the pen back was going to be gross, but he really had no other choice than to roll up his sleeve and plunge his arm deep into the mess.

SPLURGLE!

The sound was as disgusting as the goo felt, pushing through the slippery sludge. Matt had to turn his head away so that he could fish around with his whole arm buried inside the blob. Finally he found Diesel's fist and was able to pry his fingers open and grab hold of the pen.

"Uh-oh," Matt said, realizing that getting out of the goo was actually harder than pushing into it. Matt needed to hold on to the radiator with his free hand to pull himself out of the blob, which finally burped him out with a wet, sucking sound. Matt quickly wiped the pen on his pants and tossed a final look at Diesel and Skip. He took out his cell phone and snapped a picture. "Now, that's front-page news. Don't you think, Skip?"

He didn't wait for a response. He had a cartoon to draw.

38

NOWHERE TO HIDE

CRAZ DID HIS BEST TO OUTRUN THE ALIENS, which would've been a whole lot easier if he wasn't so out of shape.

"What do you guys think about a quick time-out?" he wheezed to the four creatures closing in on him.

"Qwizzle-glp!" yelled Marcia as she fired a blob of slime at Craz, which trailed through the air—a certain direct hit. At the last second Craz threw himself to the ground, causing the mess to miss and instead land with a wet *SPLORT* that encased the water fountain in a bubble of green, gooey gunk.

"Fair enough," Craz said, getting to his feet and then bolting straight into the empty gym. He really hoped

Matt had done his part and that a new cartoon would be saving his butt soon, because this running-around thing was getting old.

He scanned the gym for someplace to hide, but all he saw was a bin full of red rubber dodgeballs, which he quickly ducked behind. Peering around the corner of the bin, he watched the gym doors swing open and saw the four aliens come inside.

He was toast.

MATT RACED PAST THE GUIDANCE COUNSELOR'S office, glad that Mrs. Liefer wasn't there to hand out a detention slip for his running in the halls. He chuckled to himself, wondering what kind of detention the aliens would get for wanting to take over the school.

The pen was safely stuck in his jeans pocket, and he clutched in his hand the new cartoon he'd drawn. Unfortunately, thanks to Craz, the fire extinguisher had totally soaked the *Lantern*'s copier in foam. Matt had to find another machine—and fast.

He ran toward the teachers' lounge, hoping Craz was holding up okay.

• • •

LYING BEHIND THE DODGEBALL BIN, CRAZ KNEW
he was trapped. With the aliens edging closer, he had a
choice to make: become a green slime statue or fight his
way out of this mess.

Gary's scary hiss mixed with the awful alien stench
that was getting stronger and more disgusting. "It's now
or never," Craz tried to convince himself. "One . . . two . . .
three!"

He jumped to his feet and faced the aliens, who were
just yards away from capturing him. Marcia raised her
scepter, but Craz was quicker. He reached into the bin
and grabbed a ball, which he threw with surprising
accuracy.

WHAM! He knocked the scepter out of her fingers,
and all eyes watched it skitter across the shiny gym floor
and disappear underneath the bleachers.

"What'd you expect?" Craz shouted as he balanced
two more of the rubber balls in his hands. "Fourth-grade
dodgeball champ . . . runner-up."

The aliens were stunned. Craz was on fire, and every
ball he threw hit one of his targets. *"That's* for picking on

me in second grade.... *That's* for not inviting me to your tenth birthday party.... And *that's* for ... Uh-oh."

Craz had emptied the bin and now stood totally defenseless in the face of four really angry beings from outer space. "You know, maybe we can just talk about this," he said, and chuckled nervously as Marcia, Gary, Tommy, and Cindy were free to move closer. "I have a juice box and half a tuna sandwich in my locker. Anyone hungry?"

In response Gary snarled, showing off his razor-sharp teeth, and Tommy's arms slowly extended from his metallic body, ready to rip at Craz, who suddenly had the urgent need for a bathroom.

"Back off!" It was Matt, who had heard Craz's yelling from the hallway and had raced to the gym. Copying the cartoon would have to wait. His friend needed help. Matt was trembling on the inside, but he tried to make his voice sound deep and confidant. He still kind of squeaked. "One more step and I'll turn you all into kittens." He held the pen like it was a light saber that could strike down his opponents with one swift move. "Don't think I won't do it!"

In the moment it took for the aliens to turn and stare at Matt, Craz grabbed the empty dodgeball bin and pushed it as hard as he could, knocking them all over like intergalactic bowling pins.

"Strike!" Craz shouted as he sprinted across the gym to Matt. He gave his friend a stinging high five. "I would've been happy with a spare."

They turned to run out of the gym, but Matt suddenly couldn't move.

"Craz! My leg!"

Looking down, both boys saw that Tommy had extended one of his tentacle arms across the gym floor, and it was now clamped onto Matt's ankle. Making things worse, the arm was retracting back inside his robot body, pulling Matt with it.

"Gimme your hand," Craz yelled, trying to pull Matt

away from the alien grip. But Craz was no match for the robot's strength. Matt and the new cartoon were sliding faster toward the alien group.

It was too late to give the drawing to Craz, but Matt had another idea.

"Craz, catch!" Matt pulled the pen from his pocket and tossed it across the floor. "You know what to do." He shoved the cartoon in his other pocket.

Craz picked up the pen. "Actually, I don't have a clue. You're the cartoonist." He watched Matt get lifted by the seat of his pants.

"Just draw something that fixes this!" Matt shouted as Tommy swung him back and forth like a freshly caught fish. "Hurry!"

39

CRAZ TO THE RESCUE

CRAZ MADE IT TO THE TEACHERS' LOUNGE. HE
locked the door from the inside and caught his breath.
He had the pen. Now he just had to use it.

The first thing he did was quickly scope out the
room for essentials, which for him meant finding something to eat. Luckily, it had been Mrs. Petrone's birthday yesterday, so a slab of half-stale cake was still in
a bakery box by the sink. Craz lifted the lid, grabbed
a hunk of the vanilla-swirl cake, and snarfed it down
in one humongous bite. Braced for the sugar rush, he
picked up a few pieces of paper from the recycling bin
and then sat down at the teachers' long table, ready to
save the day.

All he had to do was draw something to stop the aliens. How hard could that be?

For Matt it would've been a cinch. He'd simply whip off a cartoon that could set things right. But Craz knew he couldn't really draw. Sure Boyd T. Boone had told him how to make a simple bike and which lines to use to draw an iguana. But actually drawing a comic that would turn four aliens back into kids? He panicked. He couldn't draw people. At all! And each time he tried to make a cartoon, the paper was just a mess of scratchy lines and ink stains. He knew it didn't have to be perfect. But without Boyd T. Boone's help, the more he tried, the worse he got.

He bounced his leg nervously as the crumpled sheets of paper piled up. He pictured poor Matt, a helpless hostage of those awful creatures, but even guilt didn't make his artistic efforts any better.

"I'm just the idea guy," he heard himself say in defeat, and then he remembered Boyd T. Boone telling him ideas are just as important as the art.

That's when he looked out the window and saw the football team still practicing in the fading afternoon light. Coach Arakanian was screaming his head off at the exhausted players, who were lined up in formation shouting over and over, "We're the Killer Bees! Killer Bees! Killer Bees!"

It was such a simple solution that Craz had to smile. *Why not?* he asked himself before grabbing a new sheet of paper and drawing something he knew he could get right.

40

BUZZ

"GARGIL-MINTEEFRESCH!" MARCIA SHRIEKED AS she paced back and forth in front of Matt, whose hands were tied behind him by one of the gym climbing ropes.

"Great speech today, Marcia," Matt said nervously. "Hey, remember that time I let you use my calculator? Good times, right?"

Behind Marcia, Gary flexed his cockroach muscles and tested his sharp claws by making ominous snips in the air. His glowing purple eyes seemed to bore holes through Matt. If Marcia hadn't been there, Matt was sure Gary would have been using his pincher claws to trim more than just his hair. But Marcia was running things, which meant Matt was safe from real harm. For now anyway.

Tommy was busy using his long tentacle arm to try to find Marcia's scepter under the bleachers. That left Cindy keeping watch by the gym door, with all three eyes scanning in opposite directions. Matt couldn't help but wonder if Cindy liked him. He didn't care if it was Cindy the girl, or Cindy the alien, as long as one of them thought he was okay.

"Frizz-u-lach!" Marcia said, and clapped her weird hands together. Tommy had just rescued her scepter, along with one high-topped red sneaker and a broken badminton racquet. Those extendable arms were really something.

While Marcia rushed to retrieve her weapon, Matt wondered what was taking Craz so long. He'd had plenty of time to draw a new cartoon. The aliens should have turned back into student council kids by now. He checked the large clock on the wall—five fifteen. In just over an hour the building would be full for parent-teacher night. If things didn't get back to normal soon . . . Matt didn't want to picture the chaos.

Suddenly Cindy started making weird screeching

noises. Something was happening in the hallway, and based on the way she was quickly scurrying away from the door, it couldn't be good.

Matt was aware of the buzzing noise before he saw what was causing it, but the sound was enough.

"Bees," Matt said as he instinctively tried to reach for the EpiPen that was hanging around his neck. Just the thought of being stung and the potential deadly effect made him cold and sweaty. And with his hands tied behind him, he instantly knew he would have no way to save himself if he got stung.

Marcia and Tommy stood in the middle of the gym, trying to figure out what was going on. Only Gary seemed excited by the sound, and he clicked his pinchers together as he ran toward the noise.

Panicked, Matt squirmed against the ropes to try to loosen the knots. At first it was painful and the rough rope burned his skin. But suddenly the rope went slack and simply slid off his wrists.

He turned around and was eye to eyes with Cindy.

Matt reached to hold her hand-paw things. "Cindy. Thank you." She smiled. At least Matt thought that's what she did. The buzzing grew deafening right before

the doors burst open and the gym filled with a blitz of giant bees.

"*Killer* bees!" shouted Craz, who was the last to arrive in the gym. He blew a coach's whistle. "Attack!"

While Matt and Craz ran from the gym, the oversize bees swarmed into formation, and then Paulie Frick ran a play that would've made Coach Arakanian proud. Even Gary's pinchers were no match for the enormous lethal stingers, which came at the aliens from every angle.

Defensively Marcia was able to score a direct hit with her scepter, dropping linebacker bee Barry Heinz to the floor in a dense green gob. But that only riled up the rest of the bee team, and if there's one thing you don't want to do to a swarm of killer bees, it's make them even madder!

The aliens didn't stand a chance.

41

BEE FREE

"KILLER BEES, CRAZ? YOU KNOW I'M ALLERGIC."
Matt was jammed inside a locker, hoping to stay hidden from the bees. "What were you thinking?"

Craz let out a long sigh. "Sorry, Matt. I forgot, okay?" He was stuffed into the locker too. The coat hook pushed painfully into his back, and there was a ripe smell that came from either someone's long-forgotten lunch or him.

"Tell me again how you thought this was a good idea?" Matt asked.

"Simple," said Craz. "Once I realized there was no way I could draw the aliens back into kids, I went with the bee idea. Basic striped circles with wingy things.

Anyone can draw that. And they're natural predators."

"But they're attacking *us*!" Matt was furious.

"Right," Craz admitted. "My bad."

BAM!

Out in the hallway the double doors shook from the impact of a bee blocker's helmet. The bees were done with the aliens in the gym. Now they were hunting Matt and Craz.

Matt fumed silently but finally spoke. "You could've killed me back there. Don't you ever think of anyone but yourself?"

"Hey, last time I looked, you aren't about to be goo-ified by aliens. How about a thank-you?"

"Thank you? What is wrong with you? You're an idiot!" Matt was glad they were separated by the metal locker wall. It kept him from choking Craz. "All you had to do was draw one thing. You couldn't even do that right."

Craz shook his head in the darkness. Matt had hit a nerve. "Hey, I'm sorry I'm not a *great artist* like you, Matt. But at least I tried to actually *do* something. Not run in the other direction. Man, you're afraid of everything!"

The hallway filled with the angry sound of the whole killer bee football team. Matt and Craz held their breaths as the buzzing grew louder and more threatening.

Looking through the ventilation slats, Matt watched as the bees swarmed past. He let out a quiet sigh of relief, but Craz had nailed it. He *was* afraid of everything, and he hated himself for it. "Hey, Principal Droon has a copy machine in his office, right?"

Craz was still mad, but he answered anyway. "Yeah. Why?"

Matt nodded. He knew what he had to do. He grabbed the pen from Craz's pocket and then flung the locker door open. Leaping into the hallway, he glanced toward the bees, who were at the far end of the hallway. Once they saw him, it was going to be a race that he had to win. Or else.

Craz cracked open his locker. "Matt, what are you doing?"

But Matt was already running down the hallway, away from the bees. Craz peeked farther out from his locker and saw the team turn around and fly after Matt, which meant they'd also just spotted him.

"Oh, man!" Craz had no choice but to slam the locker door shut and hope the bees would respect his privacy.

Fat chance.

ROUNDING THE CORNER, MATT HEARD THE BEES gaining on him and was glad to see the door to the main office. For a second he pictured Cindy. His heart sank a little, knowing that as soon as he copied the new cartoon, she wouldn't remember the smile they'd shared back in the gym. Of course, she'd be a girl again, but Matt knew liking her had never been only about what she looked like.

Matt shot into the principal's office and quickly pushed a chair against the door.

"Can I help you?" a startled Principal Droon asked Matt, who had no time to explain a thing.

First Matt unfolded the cartoon he'd already made. Sure it had been stuffed in his pocket and was all creased, but that shouldn't matter. He quickly added a new panel to it that would turn the bees back into football players. He also decided that Mrs. Bentz had probably been a pirate long enough too.

Matt ignored the angry bees battering their helmets against the barricaded door. He desperately pushed the loose pile of papers from the top of the copy machine and then opened the lid and slapped his cartoon down onto the glass.

"You are aware you're early for parent-teacher night," Principal Droon said, now crouched behind his desk. One harsh look from Matt shut him right up.

Matt fumbled with the keypad and finally calmed down enough to enter the number one for how many copies he wanted. He slammed the lid shut and then looked wildly for the button that would make the final magic happen.

"Come on, come on!" Matt shouted while he pushed different buttons on the machine, hoping he would hit the right one.

THE THREE BEES IN THE HALLWAY OUTSIDE CRAZ'S locker were really having fun.

Craz, on the other hand—not so much. The first stinger that had pierced the door had only ripped through his shirt, thankfully not turning him into a shish kebab. But the bees were persistent and took turns trying to skewer him. The stingers sliced easily through the metal, and Craz had to shift his body left and then right to try to avoid getting stung. It was just a matter of time before one of the bees got lucky, Craz thought, unaware that the three huge bees were in a huddle making a new play to all attack at once.

Craz sucked in his gut.

The bees readied their final strike.

MATT FOUND THE BUTTON.

The old copy machine rattled and hummed, and then the first blast of light shot out from under the lid.

Inside the office Matt didn't dare breathe, while a few hundred feet away a petrified Craz braced for the worst with his eyes shut tight.

And then the second burst of light filled the entire school.

42

PHEW!

"HELLO? KILLER BEES? CRAZY ALIENS?"

Craz slowly opened the locker door and made sure the coast really was clear. Thankfully, everything seemed to be back the way it was supposed to be. Everything except how he felt about Matt.

He'd been called an idiot plenty of times. But never by the guy who was supposed to be his best friend. And he still thought the bee idea was genius—if not also just *slightly* deadly.

Matt walked out of the principal's office wondering why he didn't feel better. For once he hadn't just hidden. He'd finally taken action. But the last thing he felt like was a hero. He turned into the hallway with the original cartoon in his hand and ran into a sunburned and bug-bitten Mrs. Bentz wearing a strange hat made from what looked like a huge leaf. She was holding a cutlass, which she swung haphazardly at an invisible foe.

"I know you're out there . . . Long John? Jim Hawkins? It's me. Edna!"

Instantly Matt kind of regretted bringing her back to the school, but he figured the pen had caused enough trouble for one day.

"Um, Mrs. Bentz," Matt said, being careful not to get too close. "Kilgore Junior High is a weapon-free school."

"School?" She seemed to remember the place. "Aye. That it is!" She let the cutlass drop to her side as she looked all around the hallway for familiar signs. She grabbed Matt by the collar and pulled him close, whispering, "So is this a dream too?"

"Beats me," said Matt as he pulled away, and then he rushed past her. "But it's parent-teacher night. You might want to brush your teeth."

While Mrs. Bentz stumbled toward her classroom, Matt came into the main hallway and saw Craz still standing by the lockers. He didn't know what to say but wanted to try to fix things.

"You're okay," Matt said. "That's great."

"Yeah. Great." Craz looked away. The silence felt like it went on forever. "Hey, it's almost six. I better go meet up with my parents."

"Right," Matt said. "Parent-teacher night." The pen dug into his leg, and he wished he could erase the conversation they'd had back in the lockers. "Look, Craz—"

Craz cut him off. "I really better get going, Matt. Later, okay?"

"Right," Matt said. "Later."

BY SIX FIFTEEN THE SCHOOL WAS CRAWLING WITH parents trying to follow the confusing charts plastered on the walls that showed which teachers were assigned to what classrooms. Kids led their parents around like obedient sheepdogs, for the most part dreading the night's events because they knew that no good ever comes from parents and teachers actually talking.

Matt texted his parents, saying that he was waiting for them inside the school by the front doors. He saw Craz's parents arrive and said a quick hello before watching them meet up with their son, who had chosen to wait by the cafeteria instead of by the doors with Matt.

"Oh, Larry. Wait until you hear," Mrs. Crazinski said as she gripped Craz's hands.

"Hear what?" Craz asked. But his mother just grinned and pointed to Craz's dad, who was finishing a call on his cell phone.

"That's fantastic news," Mr. Crazinski was saying to someone. "Of course I can make that happen."

He smiled at Craz and gave him a big thumbs-up. He covered the phone with his hand. "I have news," he said quietly to Craz. "Big news!" He went back to his call. "That's right, Mr. Lieber. Next week is perfect."

While his dad finished his call, Craz's mom studied the list on the wall and made notes of where all of the teachers would be. Craz could see that Matt was still waiting for his folks to show up, and for half a second he felt bad about how he'd blown off talking. But that feeling passed and was replaced by the hurt and anger, which rushed back in like a hard-hitting wave.

On a normal parent-teacher night Craz only got one parent and could only see two teachers because time was so short, divided among all the Crazinski kids. But thanks to his new, condensed family, Craz had both parents, and unfortunately their undivided attention was laser-beamed on every one of his classes.

First stop was science, where his teacher, Mr. Matthews, echoed the same thing that they were to hear from all of Craz's teachers. "Larry could try harder in class and I'm sure that would make a difference in his grades, which frankly are quite average."

"Did you hear that?" Craz excitedly asked his parents once they were back in the busy hallway. "I'm average!"

Mr. Crazinski crossed his arms. "Larry, you really are going to have to buckle down and pull your grades out of this nosedive."

"Nosedive? My grades are the same as they've always been. I'm getting all Cs. B minus in geography. That's pretty great, right?"

His parents looked at each other. His mom's smile was a bit too toothy, the way it was whenever she was excited.

"Should we tell him?" Mrs. Crazinski asked in a giddy voice that was on the verge of cracking.

Mr. Crazinski nodded. He put his right hand onto Craz's shoulder. "Son, you aren't going to believe the adventure we are about to have."

Craz stepped back. "Adventure?" Something was definitely up. He looked at his parents and now saw how different they seemed. Since when did his father wear fancy suits? And what had happened to his mother's disorganized, overflowing pocketbook and mismatched clothes that were always thrown on in a rush? "I don't think I want an adventure."

"Sorry, sport," Mr. Crazinski said with a grin Craz was sure he'd never seen before. "It's a done deal."

43

JUST LIKE OLD TIMES

MATT WAITED ALONE BY THE SCHOOL DOORS until eight o'clock. He felt like a major jerk just standing by himself in the school hallway while all the other kids he knew were being dragged around by at least one parent. Finally giving up, he wandered the hallways, sneaking glances into classrooms filled with normal-looking families, and he once again wished for something he didn't have.

At eight thirty he used his phone to send one final message: *WHERE R U!!!?*

His phone rang immediately. It was his mom. "Sweetheart, I am so sorry."

Had she been crying? Matt was pretty sure her voice

was a little drippy. "What happened to you guys? It's almost over."

And that's when his mom told him she had spent the entire evening waiting for his father. She had gotten off work early because their plan had been to come to the school together after a quick dinner downtown at a restaurant they both loved. But he kept calling from his office to say he was leaving in five minutes. "And I should know that five minutes is never five minutes. And I should have just left and come to meet you by myself, because your father . . ."

Matt knew the rest. His father was a workaholic. That had always been the problem. Even with his promises, work just consumed him and took over his brain. How many missed soccer games had his dad promised to come and watch? How many family Sundays had he simply skipped?

"It's okay, Mom," he said. "Lots of kids' parents couldn't come. My grades are fine anyway. And this thing is a huge waste of time. Trust me."

He listened as she blew her nose on the other end of the phone, and he was mad at his father all over again.

THE RED SPORTS CAR WAS PARKED IN THE

driveway, so Matt knew as soon as he stepped off the bus that his father had finally left his office. Maybe everything would be okay, he thought. But walking toward his house, he immediately knew things were bad. He could hear their fight from the street.

"What do you want me to do, Mindy? Take a pay cut?"

"No. I want you to put your kids first, David," his mother shot back. "And me."

Matt stood frozen on the front steps. He'd almost forgotten about the cramped fist in his gut that grabbed him when his parents argued this way. He instantly pictured himself much younger, rolled in a tight ball in his bed, humming so he didn't have to hear the exact words of the fight—just the dull, barking sounds of it. At least he couldn't remember the last time his stomach felt this way. That was a plus.

"I just don't understand why the family can't be as important to you as your job!" Matt's mom shouted.

"Right. And who would pay for all the nice things? The dinners out? Our vacation to the Bahamas?" his father yelled back.

"It's not about money!"

"It's always about money!"

Matt couldn't face walking through the middle of this battlefield, so he snuck around to the back door and was surprised to see Ricky at the kitchen table. He just sat there tearing a napkin into little pieces and adding the paper bits to a growing pile.

"Déjà vu all over again," Ricky said as soon as Matt sat at the table. "At least we had a few days of peace and quiet. It was kind of nice, you know?"

Matt let out a long breath. "I know." He felt the pen digging into his leg in his pocket. Why hadn't he drawn his father back in the family with a totally different job? Or given him a ton of money? Maybe that would've made everything work out better. Maybe he could still fix things by drawing something different.

"And what was that with Ricky and the guitar? You know we had talked about that before." His mother's voice was loud and firm. "Why do you always have to swoop in and be the fun parent and make me out to be the bad guy?"

"You know, Mindy, I don't know how many times we can have the same fight," the brothers heard Mr. Worfle say from the other side of the wall. "I do the best I can at being myself, and if that means being the fun one, then I'm happy to do it."

"We're supposed to be partners, David," Mrs. Worfle snapped. "It's starting to feel like we're on opposite teams."

"That's it!" Ricky stood up from the kitchen table. "Time to let my music drown this out." He turned to Matt before heading to his room. "If I were you, I'd do it too. And turn it up. Loud."

44

BIG NEWS

WHILE RICKY BLOCKED OUT THE FIGHTING beneath a pair of headphones, Matt escaped the noise by doodling. He sat at his desk, and the angry voices faded behind the random characters that soon filled his page with comforting ease. Getting lost this way was normal for Matt, and so he was surprised when the knock on his door made him realize the yelling had stopped.

"Mom wants us in the living room" was all that Ricky said.

Matt followed Ricky, expecting his mother to look upset because of the blowout with his dad. But, sitting on the couch, she didn't look miserable like all the other times they'd had their loud fights. Sad? Maybe. But not like she'd been crying, or worse. She stood up when the boys walked in.

"Matt. Ricky," she began. "Your father and I . . ."

Matt knew what was coming.

She continued. "We decided that we need a break, a little time to figure some things out."

"So Dad just took off?" Ricky asked. "For good?"

"I don't really know, Ricky. That's something he and I need to discuss."

Matt couldn't believe his dad had left them again. Well, to Matt it was happening again. For his mother and brother he'd moved out for the first time.

"He didn't even want to wait to say good-bye?" Matt asked, keenly aware that was exactly what his father had done the first time he'd walked out on them. Don't second chances ever work out?

Mrs. Worfle let out a long sigh. "Your father loves you guys. Despite how he shows it. You have to know that."

Ricky shook his head. "Look, Mom. About the guitar—"

"This isn't about the guitar, Ricky. You didn't cause this. It's been brewing for a long time."

Ricky stared at his sneakers as Matt looked at his

mother. The first time his dad walked out, she was a wreck. But now she looked like this was a change she was ready for.

BACK IN HIS ROOM MATT STARED AT THE CARTOON of his happy family. He'd thought he could fix his parents' problems with his pen and ink, but he guessed even magic couldn't change something so deeply wrong.

He tossed the cartoon into the trash.

The door opened a crack and Ricky leaned into the bedroom. "Pretty weird night," he said, looking like he wasn't sure if he should come all the way in or just close the door. "Look, I was thinking of getting some air. Maybe a quick Dairy Queen run. You in?"

Matt couldn't remember the last time Ricky had asked him to do anything. "I'm in," he said, grabbing his coat from his chair. "Totally in."

45

BROTHERS AGAIN

A SLIVER OF MOON HUNG IN THE AUTUMN SKY above the brothers, who sat on the warped picnic table to the right of the small parking lot. The DQ was a short walk from their house, and during the summer you had to stand in long lines to get what you wanted. But it was already November and they were the only customers.

"Oreo Blizzard," Ricky said as he scraped a spoonful across his bottom teeth. Even as a kid that's how he'd eaten his ice cream, and Matt liked seeing that his older brother still did it. "This takes me back."

"Yup. Nothing like a Blizzard," Matt said while chewing on a treasured chunk of cookie that he'd unearthed in his cup. "Of course, I think they taste a little better

when the weather's hot." He pulled the coat zipper up to his neck. "Not that I'm complaining."

The brothers sat silently enjoying their ice cream. Matt knew that the first time his dad walked out, Ricky had just gotten meaner. He'd barely even tolerated Matt. But something different was happening this time, and even if it didn't last, Matt was glad to be sitting in the cold, eating Blizzards with his brother.

"So," Ricky said, tossing his empty cup into the trash can. "This Dad thing. You okay?"

Matt thought about it. "Yeah," he said. "You?"

Ricky looked up at the slice of moon. He nodded slowly. "I think so." And then he added, "It's not like there's anything we can do about it anyway."

Matt scraped his spoon around his cup and then ate the last bite of ice cream. "Right," he said. "Nothing we can do at all."

46

CALLING CRAZ

WHEN THE BOYS GOT BACK HOME, THE LIGHTS were off, so they tried to be quiet tiptoeing into the kitchen. Matt expected it to feel a little weird with his father gone, but then remembered he'd been living without his dad for months. No big deal.

Ricky disappeared into his room, supposedly to do his homework, while Matt opened the fridge looking for something to eat. All he'd had for dinner was the Blizzard, and he wanted something real to top off the treat.

The kitchen light flickered on, and Matt turned to see his mom in her bathrobe. "Hungry?" she asked.

"A little," Matt said, grabbing a cold chicken leg from a plate and then closing the fridge door.

"Listen, I know a lot is going on tonight," she said, "but while you were out, I got a call from Craz's mother."

Matt felt his face tighten. "So?"

"So," his mother continued, "she wanted me to tell you. They're moving. Right away."

Moving? Matt's stomach did a backflip. "No way. Craz didn't say anything about that." And the anger rose up again. "How long has he known?"

His mother raised an eyebrow in that way that said she knew something she wasn't saying. "Just call him."

CRAZ DIDN'T WANT TO TALK TO MATT, BUT WHAT choice did he have when the Skype invite popped up on his computer?

"What do you mean you're moving?" Matt stared out from Craz's computer. "When were you going to tell me?"

"It's not like I was keeping it a secret," Craz shot back. "Besides, what do you care anyway? Oh, right. I forgot. Without me around, no one's going to tell you what to do with your life."

The two boys just stared into their computers for a

moment. Matt bit his thumbnail. Craz shook his head.

"For the record," Craz began, "I found out tonight. My dad got some promotion thing. We leave in two days. It's crazy. I mean, Shanghai, China? Who moves to China?"

Craz slumped over onto his desk out of sight of the webcam, so Matt had to deal with talking to the iguana, who was parked on top of Craz's head.

"Two days?" Matt drummed his fingers on his desk. He wasn't sure what to say or how to feel. "What about your brothers and sisters? What do they think?"

Craz slowly rose up into the picture on Matt's computer. There was something odd about the look on his face.

"About that," Craz began. He took a deep breath and then looked right into the webcam. "I think I'm an only child."

"What? No, you're not. I mean, you always *wished* you were an only child, but . . ." Matt leaned forward so that his face was now huge on Craz's computer. "Craz, what did you do?" And then it hit him. "No. What did you *draw*?"

Craz reached off camera and then sheepishly held up the cartoon he'd made.

Matt studied it for a second. "That's you taking a shower. So?"

"So . . . the pen screwed it up. All I wanted was time to think in the shower. I should've just drawn a giant hot water tank!"

"The pen didn't screw it up, Craz. You did." Matt instantly got what happened. "Typical. You didn't think it through. You just gave yourself more shower time. Of course that could mean less kids in the family."

"Tell me something I don't know," Craz snapped. "Obviously it's not what I planned, Matt. You think I like all these changes around here? My mom is like a gourmet chef now. . . . Okay. That change I can handle."

Matt remembered too many terrible meals at Craz's house. "I just wish you'd think things through. Look at the mess you've made."

"Fine. It's all my fault. Are you happy?"

Matt didn't say anything. He wasn't happy. In fact, he was still pretty mad.

"Look, I get what I did." Craz said. "Just because I like to space out under a nice hot stream of pulsating water, now I have to learn to eat with chopsticks!" Craz grabbed the webcam from his computer and held it right up to his face. "I can't deal with chopsticks, Matt. You've got to fix this. Tonight!"

"*I've* got to fix it? I didn't get you into this mess."

Craz let out a sigh. "Please, Matt. I goofed up, okay? I don't know what to do."

"Fine." Matt pulled the pen from his pocket. His first thought was that he should use it to fix his own family. But he'd already tried that. And nothing had really changed.

"I'll redraw you with all your sibs and make sure your dad's job still bites. And your mom is back to being a kitchen disaster."

"Right. All that stuff," Craz said. He paused. "But can you keep the big-screen TV? And Virgil?"

Matt slowly nodded. He took the cap off the pen. "Chopsticks, no. Big-screen TV and iguana, yes."

Matt grabbed a sheet of paper and thought for a second about the cartoon he needed to draw to make sure Craz didn't have to move halfway around the world. He chewed on the pen cap for a second and then shook his hand the way he always did to get the juices flowing before he started to draw.

He put the sharp tip of the pen onto the paper and made the first line. But instead of that exciting moment when the black ink flowed onto the paper, nothing happened. No ink came out.

"Uh-oh," Matt said.

"What do you mean 'uh-oh'?" Craz asked. "'Uh-oh' doesn't sound good."

Matt tried the pen again, but again nothing came out. He quickly unscrewed the shaft from the pen and frowned when he saw that the plastic container inside was empty. "I think we used up all the ink at school."

"So fill it back up," Craz said. "No biggie, right?"

Matt grabbed the fancy ink bottle with the cork stopper that had come with the cartooning kit. He opened it and peered into the dark well. He gasped. "Uh, I think it's a big problem," Matt said as he tipped the little bottle upside down. He stared into the webcam. His face was pale. "There's no more ink. I can't make a new cartoon."

47

WHERE'S BOYD?

MATT AND CRAZ SET TO WORK IMMEDIATELY, searching their computers to try to find the cartooning website that had first introduced them to Boyd T. Boone and his amazing kit. They had to find more ink, or Craz would be gone. It was as simple as that. Not that Matt wasn't ready to ship Craz out of town himself, but—well, it just didn't seem right that it was happening like this.

But no matter what search words they tried—and they tried every word combination they could think of—neither could find the Draw Better Now web page anywhere on the Internet.

As the sleepless night wore on, Matt attempted to make the magic work by filling the pen with some regular drawing ink that he had lying around, which did nothing but clog the pen and stain the carpet. Craz even forced Matt to re-create the mess that Craz had made on Matt's keyboard, to see if spilled pizza-pocket sauce might somehow have helped them stumble onto the website.

"No luck, Craz," Matt said, too tired to even care that his keyboard was now totally sloppy. "It's almost like that website never existed."

Craz was totally freaking out. It was four o'clock in the morning. A moving company that his dad's business hired was going to show up at his house in three hours and start packing everything they owned into boxes that would follow them the next day to China. For a second he imagined that with five kids in the family the movers would sure use up a ton of boxes. But then he remembered it was just him—and suddenly he really missed his sisters and brothers. He wished he could have a fight with Pete or get an earful of Hank's dumb advice or plop down in Becca's room and let little Meagan bounce around the bed on top of him while he told them both his problems. But of course his problems were the reason that he didn't have any brothers or sisters anymore. It was probably the reason he didn't have a best friend anymore too.

"MATT! WAKE UP!" CRAZ SHOUTED THROUGH the computer.

Matt opened his eyes and sat back up so that his groggy face was looking out from Craz's computer screen. "What is it? Did you find the website?"

Craz shook his head. "No, but I've got a new idea, and it's going to take both of us to make it work!"

THE PLAN WAS SIMPLE. AS SOON AS THE SUN came up, the boys were going to split up and search all the places around town where they'd had encounters with Boyd T. Boone. And once they found the cartoonist, he'd definitely hook them up with more ink, and then every-thing would be okay.

Matt still had to go to school, so that was his territory. And since Craz had already been given the day off to help pack, he'd skip out of the house and bike around town, checking out all the other places the weird cartoonist had been spotted.

Sure it was a long shot, but they were running out of options . . . and time.

Matt didn't even bother going to sleep. He waited until a decent hour and then went to school early and immediately checked out the cafeteria, where Craz had seen Boyd T. Boone wearing a hairnet and running the cash register. Unfortunately, the only people he could find there were the usual assortment of lunch ladies, who were busy preparing mysterious vats of supposedly edible options for that day's lunch. No plump bald man with a bushy mustache.

Defeated, Matt sat through two classes before work-ing up the courage to do the unthinkable—going to Principal Droon's office. No kid in the history of Kilgore Junior High took it on her- or himself to go see the principal without first being summoned there for some sort of discipline issue. But Matt was on a mission, so he combed back his hair, made sure his shirt was tucked in, and then walked into the school office unannounced.

"Yes? Can I help you?" Mrs. Tisch, the bone-thin school secretary, asked from behind the long counter in the outer office. She sounded mad even though Matt hadn't said anything yet.

"I'd like to see the principal, please," Matt said. "It's an emergency."

"Emergency! Do I need to dial 911?" Mrs. Tisch had the look of someone who really wanted to make the call.

"Uh, no. It's not that kind of emergency," Matt said. "But it's important. Really important."

Disappointed, Mrs. Tisch let out a loud sigh and then motioned for Matt to come around the counter. She led the way to the closed office door behind her. "Make it fast," she said. "Principal Droon is a *very* busy man."

She knocked on the door and then opened it before waiting for a response. The secretary pushed Matt into the room, where he stood staring at the startled face of his dreaded principal, who had his shirtsleeves rolled up

and was jumping around the tidy office with a Wii con-
troller in his hand.

"Uh, I thought I said no interruptions," Principal
Droon said as he quickly turned off the TV, where his
kung fu game had been playing.

"Emergency," Mrs. Tisch said flatly while she backed
out of the room and closed the door.

Principal Droon tried to look serious, but even he
knew it was way too late for that. He crossed his arms
and sat on the corner of his desk, but to Matt he was more
sweaty than threatening. "What's this about, Mr. . . . ?"

"Worfle. Matt Worfle, sir." Matt relaxed a little as he pushed on. "I'm looking for a teacher—a substitute, actually. For Mrs. Bentz. Yesterday. Big guy? Bushy mustache? Boyd T. Boone?"

The principal nodded like he totally knew who Matt was talking about, but then he said, "I think you're a little mixed up. Mrs. Bentz's sub was Nancy Fitzsimmons. I called her in myself. Retired teacher. Must be over seventy now but was a real firecracker in her day. What's this about anyway?"

Matt was stunned. He was positive that Boyd T. Boone had been the substitute but realized this was probably just another way that the mysterious cartoonist had disappeared without a trace.

"It's just that I, uh, really enjoyed the class," Matt lied. "I wanted to send her a thank-you letter for the, um, educational enrichment."

Principal Droon smiled. "It's refreshing to meet a student who appreciates a good thing when he sees one."

Matt just stared back with the growing sick feeling that there was nothing more he could do.

48

THE SEARCH
CONTINUES

WITH FOUR MOVERS BUSY WRAPPING THINGS
in wads of paper and putting them in carefully labeled
overseas boxes and a mother who was on the phone
making plans with a foreign real estate agent, Craz easily
slipped out of the house unnoticed. He sped into town on
his rocket-powered bike, hoping beyond hope that Boyd
T. Boone would be at one of the three places he needed
to look.

His first stop was Copy-Copy, where Mr. Hupt was
busy trying to fix a paper jam in the big color copier that
had, as usual, just broken down in the middle of a job.
Craz stood at the counter and, because he couldn't see
Mr. Hupt behind the large machine, thought it was

possible that the man would stand up and—TA-DA! It would be Boyd T. Boone.

"Just a second," the voice called out as a hammer repeatedly clanked against something metallic.

Waiting was never something Craz was good at, but right now it was actually painful for him. His foot kicked at the worn-out tiles on the floor, and he picked at a hangnail, feeling like he was going to explode. "Excuse me, but this will only take a second."

He instantly stopped fidgeting as the man slowly rose from behind the copy machine, wiping his hands on a dirty rag.

"Now, what can I do for you today?"

Craz's hopeful smile dropped. It was just Mr. Hupt, who had no idea who this Boyd T. Boone character was and looked at Craz like he was crazy when he tried to explain that he'd actually talked to the man right there behind the counter.

Strike one, Craz thought as he got back onto his bike and then rocketed off to Easel & Brush to check out the art store's delivery guy.

Rushing down the street with the booster blaring, he

couldn't help but feel sad that he really might have to leave the town where he had spent his whole life. And why? Because he liked long showers.

"Matt's right. I am an idiot," he said as he safely flew through the intersection and into the Easel & Brush parking lot.

First he checked with the store manager and made sure that there was only one delivery person and that was Frankie, the cranky guy who had dropped the drawing table off at Matt's house the day that Boyd T. Boone had appeared in the van. That was the good news.

The bad news: Frankie had no clue who Boyd T. Boone was and swore that he was the only one who ever drove the van. In fact, he was the only one who had a set of keys.

Strike two.

Craz slumped back onto his bike and didn't even engage the rocket, choosing instead to pedal across town toward his last chance to find Boyd T. Boone—the restaurant where Matt had eaten with his family, Casa Cubana.

"Sorry, kid," said Juan Carlos, the waiter who Matt

said had mysteriously become Boyd T. Boone. "I'm the only me I know. Sounds like your friend is *loco*."

Craz ducked as a second waiter brought a large tray of garlic chicken platters out from the kitchen. "My friend isn't crazy. This guy, he just kind of pops up."

Juan Carlos waved at two new customers and pointed to a small corner table. He turned back to Craz. "I wish I could help you, my amigo. Sorry."

Normally Craz would grab an order to go and sit out-

side on the curb enjoying the tasty lunch. But today wasn't normal.

He had to accept the facts: The pen was still out of ink and he was out of ideas.

Strike three.

49

GOOD-BYE

THE NEXT DAY A HUGE MOVING VAN WAS PARKED in front of Craz's house. The wide double doors at the back were open, and the sweaty movers struggled to get an antique bureau up the metal ramp and safely inside. Packed boxes were stacked in different-size piles on the lawn, and several more movers made trip after trip into the house, trying to get everything out and loaded up.

Craz sat on the front steps watching as his life was carried past him. He kept a hand on the one box he was most nervous about losing—his comic books.

"Our flight's at two, which means we have to be out of here no later than ten," Mr. Crazinski said as he made room for one of the movers to edge past him with another sealed box. "Is this exciting or what?"

"No, Dad," Craz said, staring down at his sneakers. "This is just awful."

Mr. Crazinski bent down, being careful not to crease his shiny pants. "Look, Larry, I know it seems like a big deal. You're moving away from everything you know. But trust me, you'll get over there and we'll start a new

 life and you'll forget all about this place. I promise."

"But I don't want to forget about this place. I want to stay here." Craz stood up and looked into his father's face, searching for the other father

he knew. The one who liked his crappy job and his huge family and his life on this street inside this house. "You know what, Dad?" Craz said. "I liked you a whole lot better before." He shook his head and went back inside.

"Before?" his father asked. "Before what?"

* * *

MATT'S MOTHER TOLD HIM TO GO TO SCHOOL

late. "I don't know what's up with you and Craz, but you have to say good-bye. It's the right thing to do."

"I guess," Matt muttered as he slowly got dressed to face the inevitable.

Matt grabbed his coat from behind the kitchen door and then left his house and followed the same route that he'd taken hundreds—no, *thousands*—of times. He walked down the sidewalk past the mailbox where Craz had once accidentally lost his favorite hat when he'd tried to mail it to himself. Across the street Matt passed Old Lady Hampshire's place and smiled, remembering how she'd always pay them with warm cookies when they shoveled her walkway in the winter. There was the curb that he'd crashed his bike into, breaking an arm. Craz had been the one to go get help. The memories were in every sidewalk crack and street sign, and Matt wondered how he'd ever be able to walk around the neighborhood without feeling heavy inside.

He got to Craz's house just as the last boxes were being loaded from the house into the van. Craz stood in the driveway looking as miserable as Matt felt.

"You made it," Craz said. "I wasn't sure."

"I wasn't so sure either."

They stood quiet for a second, both looking down at the asphalt. They'd been friends for almost ten years. How could being angry at each other for just a few days wipe all of that away?

"Look," Matt said, searching for the words. "I know I said some mean things . . ."

"Yeah, you did." Craz paused. "But . . . you weren't off base." He finally looked at Matt. "Who forgets his best friend's kryptonite? Bees. What was I thinking?"

Matt nodded. "And what you did? It *was* pretty awesome. Seeing the whole football team attack the aliens. Totally out there. I have to give you that."

Craz grinned. "I guess 'out there' is kind of what I do best. That's what gets me into trouble, though. I think I might be a little nuts."

"A little?" Matt almost smiled. "I could use some of that nutty side." He paused, then looked at Craz. "I'm going to miss that."

"We did make a pretty good team," Craz said. "Batman

and Robin . . . if Batman was always messing things up and Robin was afraid of his own shadow."

Matt laughed. "Yeah, just like that. Hey," he added, trying to sound cheery. "Maybe it won't be so bad over there. You can still make up weird stories, right?"

Craz nodded. "Yup. Who knows? Maybe I'll even run into some kid who likes to doodle."

They tried to smile. It was really hard.

One of the movers walked out of the garage carrying a tall box of garden tools—rakes, shovels, a hose. The garage was the last thing to be packed, and then it really was over.

"I was thinking that the only good thing about moving to Shanghai is that I don't have to hand in that lame *Treasure Island* research paper for Mrs. Bentz," Craz said. "Looks like you're on your own for that one."

"Stupid assignment," Matt said, remembering it was due tomorrow. "And it was your fault too. You left the cartoon in the copier for her to find."

"Hey, don't blame me. You were the one who drew it."

Another mover wheeled Craz's rocket bike past the boys and into the van just as Mr. and Mrs. Crazinski came out the front door and locked the house for the last time. They walked toward their car parked on the street.

"So . . . ," Matt said.

"Right . . . ," said Craz.

Mr. Crazinski honked the horn. It was time.

"I hope you don't mind," Craz said, "but I kept the copy of that first magic cartoon. Even though the cartooning kit made the mess we're in, we had fun, right?" He reached into his backpack and pulled out the copy of the "Cartoon Kings" comic.

Matt looked at the cartoon that had showed them the power of the pen and the ink. "Yeah, we had lots of fun."

"You can have the original. Once you hand in the paper, I'm sure Mrs. Bentz will give it back."

"Larry! Let's go!" Mrs. Crazinski yelled from the car.

Craz nodded to Matt, who gave him a little salute.

Matt watched the best friend he ever had walk away. He almost felt like crying but refused to let it happen. Instead he took his mind off what was happening by thinking again about the cartooning kit and the wonderful day when they first found out about the magic. He closed his eyes and pictured the "Cartoon Kings" comic and smiled. He let his mind wander from panel to panel, past the goofy way he'd drawn the two of them, past the image of the bag of money, past the drawings of the pen and the ink . . .

The PEN AND THE INK!

"Craz!" Matt shouted just as the car door closed and the car started to pull away from the curb. "I think I can fix this!"

Craz rolled down the window. "How?"

He watched out the back window as Matt ran up the metal ramp and into the moving van. A second later he reappeared sitting unsteadily atop Craz's rocket-powered bike.

"Just trust me, okay?" Matt yelled as he adjusted the helmet. He took a deep breath and started pedaling awkwardly down the street. And once he was sure he wasn't going to fall over, he flipped the red switch above the water bottle and held on for the ride of his life.

50

WILD RIDE

"WHOOOOOOAAAA!"

Matt couldn't help but scream as the rocket bike zig-
zagged wildly down the street. His face felt stretched by
the force of the ride, and he had to use every ounce of
strength and concentration to keep from crashing into
other moving objects—and there were a lot of those.
Pedestrians. Cars. Barking dogs that tried to chase after
him but quickly got lost in his dust.

"Hold. On. Tight," he said aloud as the bike bounced
over bumps and dodged potholes. He knew he had to be
careful if he wanted to make his plan work. He had to
arrive at school in one piece, not in an ambulance.

The solution to their ink problem had been at the

school all along. Matt had drawn a bottle of ink and the pen in the very first cartoon he and Craz had made. And now the original of that cartoon was locked inside Mrs. Bentz's desk. He only had to make a copy of it, and then he'd have more ink *and* another pen.

"Look out! Please! Out of the way!" Matt was approaching a stop sign and realized he didn't actually know how to safely stop the bike without flying over the handlebars.

Matt shot through the intersection just as a red sports car screeched to a stop at the corner.

"Matt?" Mr. Worfle shouted as the bike whizzed past him.

Matt saw the blur that was his father and cringed

thinking that he had drawn him that fancy car. That was another thing he planned to redraw.

Up ahead a garbage truck started to back out of an alley, and Matt heard the warning *beep-beep-beep* as the rear end of the truck edged into the street. The school was just a block past the truck, and so he gripped the handlebars tightly and angled the bike toward the space between the end of the truck and a parked car. It was a narrow space that was quickly getting narrower. He almost closed his eyes but knew that was just suicide.

ZOOM! He steered perfectly through the gap. Now the school was straight ahead and coming up fast. Matt decided to cut the rocket engine and glide the rest of the way, but when he flipped the red switch down, the booster didn't shut off. He tried it again, and this time the red switch broke off in his fingers.

"Not good!" Matt yelled as he rocketed toward his school.

With a bit more skill than he thought possible, Matt aimed the speeding bike around a school bus, whipped into the Kilgore Junior High driveway, and then took a sharp corner and flew around to the back of the school. Speeding past classroom windows, he realized he was doing a pretty decent job steering in and out of the teachers' parked cars and dodging screaming kids who came outside from the gym. He even kind of liked the ride.

"Uh-oh!"

Still full throttle, the bike jumped the low curb at the edge of the parking lot and landed, skidding, on the football field, where the tires spat out patches of grass and mud clumps as Matt roared down the field toward the huddled Killer Bee squad in the middle of a pregame practice.

"Out of the way!" he screamed. "Can't stop!"

The Killer Bees broke apart just as Matt shot past the team.

"No way," Paulie Frick said to his equally stunned teammates. "That kid is pretty cool."

Matt picked several bugs out of his teeth while he tried to figure out how he was going to stop the bike. And that's when he saw a row of low bushes about one hundred yards away. Figuring leaves and sticks were softer than pavement, he aimed the bike straight at the shrubs, closed his eyes, and jumped.

"Ahhhhhhh!"

It felt like slow motion as Matt flew through the air, before crashing hard into the middle of the pointy foliage.

His heart was pounding and he had scratches all

over his arms and he could swear some itchy leaves were stuck in his underpants, but he felt great. "That was amazing!" he shouted as he pulled himself out of the bushes and brushed himself off. And even with the football team rushing over to pat him on the back and tell him how truly awesome he was, he had a job to do, and he ran off to the side entrance and disappeared inside the school.

51

PEN AND INK

IT WAS THE MIDDLE OF THIRD PERIOD SO THE hallway was empty, which made Matt's sprint down the corridor a breeze. He was going to fix the problems— he felt it deep inside, and that thought brought a huge smile to his face.

"Watch it!"

Matt heard the cry before he saw the kid carrying a huge stack of purple paper. But it was too late.

WHAM!

The collision sent a cloud of purple pages into the air, which fluttered down all over the hallway. Matt was sprawled on his butt, and it took him a second before he realized who he'd crashed into.

"Cindy? I am so sorry," he said while trying to help gather up the scattered sheets. "Totally my fault. Totally." He stuffed a handful of paper into her arms.

"What's the big rush, Matt? Just flunk a test or something?" She was smiling. She wasn't mad, not even a little.

"It's a long story," he said as he helped Cindy to her feet. "I'll tell you about it sometime."

"Promise?"

He grinned. "Yup. I promise. In fact," he said, and took a deep breath, "you want to maybe do something sometime? You know, a movie or just hang out?"

"Do something, huh?" Cindy looked away and paused

long enough for Matt's stomach to flip over twice. "Sure. Sounds fun."

"Cool!" Matt said as he picked up the last of the purple sheets and then ran off down the hallway toward Mrs. Bentz's classroom. Out of breath, Matt got to the door and peered in the window, unprepared for what he saw. Mrs. Bentz was pacing behind her desk, which now was decorated to look like the prow of a boat with a mast made from a broom handle and a white towel stretched to be the sail. She wore wide-legged purple pantaloons with a loose white blouse and had tied a green kerchief around her head.

"Actually the island isn't as rugged as I had imagined," she was saying to her class. "And who would think that Long John Silver was such a good dancer?"

Matt burst into the room, causing Mrs. Bentz to reach to her side and hold up a cardboard sword that she pointed directly at him.

"Avast ye, lubber!" she shouted. "Stand down, I say!"

Matt had to smirk at the ridiculous sight but had no time to play pirates. "Sorry, Mrs. Bentz, but this is an emergency." He ran past her, suffering a few jabs of her cardboard sword in the process, and then rushed behind her desk and started opening the drawers.

"Hey! That's my boat—er, desk," Mrs. Bentz shouted as she did her best to pull Matt back.

The students totally got into the scuffle, and they started hooting and clapping.

"Fight! Fight! Fight!"

Matt swatted Mrs. Bentz off him and finally managed to open the bottom drawer, where all of her files were stored. He rifled through them until he came to a folder crammed with kid artwork that she had obviously been confiscating over the years. He emptied the folder on the desk.

"Matthew Worfle, I hereby give you a last warning. Cease what you are doing or suffer the consequences!"

Consequences. *That was a good one*, thought Matt, knowing how much everything affects everything else. *Sometimes one small doodle can send your entire world spinning crazily out of control.*

"Yes!" Matt spotted the "Cartoon Kings" comic. He grabbed it and turned to his teacher. "Arghhh, you make a fine pirate, Mrs. B!"

She blushed and began to thank Matt for the compliment, but he was already gone.

This time Matt didn't care who saw him inside the teachers' lounge. He quickly cut out the image of the ink bottle and magic pen from the original "Cartoon Kings" comic and then slapped the two drawings onto the copy machine.

Even though his heart was racing, he paused. What if this idea didn't work? Maybe the magic only happened one time with each cartoon, and they'd already copied the original once. *If it doesn't work now,* Matt thought, *what other options are there?*

Sadly he knew that answer. Without Boyd T. Boone's help he and Craz would be stuck with life just the way it was. For better or worse. And if Craz really did move halfway around the world, it was definitely the worst ever.

Matt closed the lid and pushed the start button. The machine made the familiar whirring noise. A second later the bright flash of light burst out from under the lid. Matt held his breath.

And then came the second flash of light.

Matt turned around, scanning the countertops for the magic pen and ink. Dirty coffee cups, half-eaten bagels, and a newspaper crumpled into a ball were all that he saw. His stomach felt sick until his eyes fell on the long table. There, sticking out from under a year-old fashion magazine, he saw the tip of a pen that looked like it *could be* his. He ran to the table and quickly lifted up the magazine, revealing a perfect copy of the pen and a full bottle of ink.

"Yes!" Matt felt relaxed for the first time in a couple of days.

Sitting at the table, Matt used the new pen and bottle of ink to draw the cartoon that would put Craz's family back together and make sure Craz didn't move away. He was actually nervous and had to start over twice. But he finally felt he'd gotten it right.

Matt placed the cartoon on the copy machine and closed the lid, confident—or at least hopeful—that everything was going to work out fine.

And then he pushed the button and waited for the twin flashes of light that would bring his best friend home.

52

BACK TO NORMAL

THE NEXT DAY BEGAN AS USUAL, WITH CRAZ getting the cold end of the shower and then having to fight over the last piece of burned French toast.

"Hands off, Becca. I put dibs on it."

"Oh, please," his sister snapped at him. "You can't dibs a piece of food."

"Well, I licked it," Meagan said. "Does that count?"

"Good ploy, Meg." Hank was at the sink washing his plate. "And, Larry, can you please clean up your side of our room? I nearly broke a toe on that plastic penguin of yours."

"My penguin!" Pete shouted as he dumped orange juice on his head. "I want it! Mine! Mine! Mine!"

Mrs. Crazinski dashed into the kitchen with a towel wrapped around her wet hair, looking frantically for her purse. Mr. Crazinski honked the horn to get everyone to hurry up, and Becca grabbed the wrong lunch bag, leaving everyone else to argue over who was going to have to eat the liver sandwich.

The noise was loud, the activity chaotic, and Craz leaned back in his chair wondering how he ever thought he could live without it.

AT SCHOOL THE MORNING WAS A SERIES OF DULL classes that Matt and Craz suffered through just so they could get to lunch period.

"Thanks again, Matt," Craz said through a huge mouthful of liver.

"No sweat, Craz. You'd do the same for me. Right?"

"Absolutely. Of course if it were me, I'd know how to use the brakes on the bike." He sighed. "It really blew up when it smashed into the wall?"

"Sorry about that part." Then Matt smiled. "But I have to admit, it was a pretty awesome ride."

"I knew you had it in you." Craz sipped his chocolate milk, anxious to get back to the new project they'd come up with last night, just hours after Craz had been zapped out of his airplane seat and back into his normal messy, overcrowded life.

"Hey," Craz said, pointing at Matt's lunch. "You're eating a Wednesday sandwich. Today is Friday."

Matt swallowed a bite of roast beef. "Yup. Gotta take some chances, right?"

Skip Turkle plopped down at the lunch table and grabbed one of Craz's potato chips. "Boys, this is your lucky day," he said, chewing with his mouth wide open.

"If this was my lucky day, Turkle, you wouldn't be sitting here." Matt could still picture the newspaper editor stuck in a blob of alien slime. It made him happy.

"Good one," Skip said, forcing one of his snortlike laughs before he tried to snag another chip from Craz without success. "Here's the deal. The *Lantern* is looking for some fresh blood on the comics page."

"What about Diesel?" Matt asked with a raised eyebrow.

"Strangest thing. He's been acting all weird the last few days, like he's afraid of something. Says he's done cartooning."

"Just like that?" Craz couldn't hide the smirk on his face.

Skip shrugged. "Just like that."

"Funny thing is," said Craz, "if you'd asked us a week ago, we'd probably have walked on hot coals at the chance. Right, Matt?"

"That's true," Matt said. "But we have our own plans now. There are other ways to get our cartoons shown around here."

Skip laughed. "Right. And how exactly are you two losers going to swing that?"

Just then Len and Sammy came by the table. "Loved the cover idea for your comic book, guys." Len slapped the full-page cartoon down on the table. "Rocket bicycles . . . killer bees . . . aliens. You've got it all!"

"Aliens?" Skip grabbed the comic book cover with the bold title that read *Crazy Times Comix*. He scoffed at how lame he thought it looked. But when his eyes fell on the drawing of the four familiar creatures from outer space, an inexplicable chill ran down his spine and Skip left the table so quickly that he knocked over his chair.

"That was fun," said Craz.

"Way fun!" Matt grinned.

* * *

AFTER MANAGING TO STAY AWAKE DURING HEALTH
class, Craz and Matt walked into English, dreading
having to tell Mrs. Bentz they didn't have their *Treasure
Island* reports. Luckily, Mrs. Bentz hadn't arrived yet,
so they took their seats and were both surprised when
Principal Droon entered the room.

"Okay. Settle down. I have an announcement to
make." Principal Droon flicked the lights on and off to
get everyone's attention, like they were in third grade.
"That's better. I'm sorry to tell you that Mrs. Bentz will no
longer be teaching you."

The room erupted in a chorus of shouts and cheers.

Paulie Frick shot his hand into the air. "What happened? Did she crack up? Were we too much for her?"

The class laughed, which didn't change Principal
Droon's expression from one of patient disgust. "All I
know is that she said she was selling her condo to go live
on an island somewhere. Not that I can make any sense
of that decision.

"In the meantime," he continued, "I've managed
to find a permanent replacement who comes highly

recommended and should be able to pick up right where Mrs. Bentz left off."

Groans filled the room as Principal Droon motioned to the door, and in walked the new teacher. He was confident. He was large. He was Boyd. T. Boone. But instead of wearing the wild beret and huge sunglasses like when he'd been their substitute teacher, now he was dressed in a normal corduroy blazer and black slacks. He actually looked like a teacher.

"They're all yours, Mr. Boone," the principal said with a dismissive wave of his hand. "Good luck."

Matt and Craz couldn't stop staring as their new English teacher unpacked his worn leather briefcase without a hint of knowing who the two boys were. The teacher sat down on the corner of the desk, facing the class. He looked so serious as he picked up a copy of *Treasure Island* and flipped through the pages.

"I hear you've been engrossed in this fine piece of

classic literature," he said. "Well, it certainly is a rollicking adventure of a book. It's got pirates. It's got treasure. But should it be the only book you read all year?" Boyd T. Boone closed the book with a sharp slap. "I don't think that's fair to you or all the other books in the world."

A small cheer rose from the students.

"That's why starting today your new assignment is to read any book you want. Think of all the great stories out there that are just waiting to be told. The possibilities are endless!"

Matt and Craz weren't sure, but it felt like that last line was delivered straight to them.

THE LAST BELL OF THE DAY FINALLY RANG, AND the hallway filled with kids who couldn't wait to get out of the building. Matt loaded up his backpack while Craz stood by his locker, wondering if they'd done the right thing with the pen.

"So you really flushed all the ink down the toilet? You didn't keep enough to even draw us some quick cash maybe?"

"Sorry," Matt said, slamming his locker shut. "But we

agreed last night. We're better off just doing things the old way. Same crazy cartoons, less mess."

"If you say so." Craz grinned. "But I'll miss the mess. . . . Well, some of it anyway."

The boys walked down the hall toward the bright afternoon sunlight. "Which reminds me," Craz continued. "What do you think of a whole comic book about pirates?"

Matt's face lit up. "Mutant space pirates!"

"Yeah, who bury cyber treasure . . . on meteors!"

"Wait," Matt said. "Does it have to be meteors?"

"You have another idea?"

Matt clapped a hand onto Craz's shoulder. "Always!"

ALAN SILBERBERG

has been looking at the world through cartoon glasses ever since he could hold a pen, and his doodles have appeared on everything from napkins to animations. He was the 2011 recipient of the SCWBI Sid Fleischman Humor Award for *Milo: Sticky Notes and Brain Freeze*, and he is also the author of the novel *Pond Scum* and the writer of numerous TV shows for Nickelodeon and Disney. Alan has a BA in Cartoon-Communication Education from the University of Massachusetts and a Masters of Education from Harvard. A former Bostonian, Alan lives with his family in Montreal, where he still roots for the Red Sox.

"Sometimes you turn to the first page of a book and you instantly know that you're going to want to read it through to the end. That's how Milo was for me." —Elizabeth Bird, Fuse 8 blog

"Milo is a treasure." —Bookpage

★ "This is more than just another funny story about a middle-school misfit . . . With Milo, the author [molds] the humor with poignancy to create a profound slice of one boy's life."

—*School Library Journal*, starred review